Books by Jacqueline Gay Walley

'Venus As She Ages' Collection of Novels:

Strings Attached (Second Edition, Gay Walley)

To Any Lengths

Prison Sex

The Bed You Lie In

Write, She Said

Magnetism

Books by Gay Walley

Novels:

Strings Attached (First Edition)

The Erotic Fire of the Unattainable

Lost in Montreal

Duet

E-Books on Bookboon:

The Smart Guide to Business Writing

How to Write Your First Novel

Save Your One Person Business From Extinction

Amazon Chap-Books:

How to Be Beautiful

How to Keep Calm and Carry On Without Money

THE BED YOU LIE

THE BED YOU LIE IN

A NOVEL

Jacqueline Gay Walley

PUBLICATIONS

Book Four of the VENUS AS SHE AGES *Collection*

I have lived many of the places I write about, many of these characters are based on real people, alive or dead. But this book is a work of fiction, because all the events and places got transmuted into a story that the real people would not even recognize. In addition, just as many of the characters are fictitious, the events are fictitious, perhaps even my analyses in the books are fictitious. That said, it bears repeating that nothing in the novel is intended as a recounting of actual events. Apart from the broad parallels, this is not what actually happened to me, nor to the people I write about.

Copyright © 2021 by Jacqueline Gay Walley
www.gaywalley.com

Published by IML Publications LLC
www.imlpublications.com

Distributed worldwide by Ingram Content Group
www.ingramcontent.com

Book cover design by Erin Rea
www.erinreadesign.com

Interior layout by Medlar Publishing Solutions Pvt Ltd, India
www.medlar.in

Cover Image: Alamy T3PTBN
'Crouching Venus' (Roman Antonine period, 2nd century AD)

ISBN: 978-1-955314-17-6

Library of Congress Control Number: 2021941312

IML Publications LLC
151 First Avenue
New York City, NY 10003

This book is dedicated to all of us
who got freed of our pain the hard way.

ONE

Maybe Arieh was right. I was nasty in bed.

"You mean last night?" I asked as I put on my dress and looked around for my sandals underneath piles of his shirts and t-shirts crumpled on the floor. There were piles everywhere— on his chest of drawers, on his air conditioner, on side tables; DVDs, coins, everything a mess, full of dust, tilted, it seemed, like a Soutine painting.

"I was depressed," I explained, buttoning up my blouse. And who wouldn't be? I thought, looking around this chaotic, filthy room. Is this a man a woman should want to be with?

"You were pugnacious," he replied.

I tried to remember when I had been pugnacious, as he called it, and all I could think was that maybe he was referring to my pushing him away. I do that in bed when I am restless.

I kissed him quickly once on his balding head while he was looking for his eyeglasses and then rushed out of there, hair uncombed, handbag open, before we could get into a wrangle.

I took a taxi home, which I could ill afford, since I live as close to the edge financially as I do in my choice of men. I was working in a tiny media company that paid less than any job I'd ever had, and had the gall to pay late. This was not perhaps the most terrible thing since, after all, it was still some income, but my inability to live within a budget of any kind was the real problem. The government and I finally had something in common.

When I got home I immediately changed into slacks and a sweater, and hurried to a subway so I could meet my boss for our weekly summit meeting at a coffee shop on the Upper West Side. At these meetings, we'd go over a list of diminishing clients and what I was doing for them, while I ate a fruit salad and she ate egg whites, and she promised me a fantastically

wealthy future once the money came in. At this convivial breakfast where we mostly talked about our love lives, politics, and
then, reluctantly, the clients, I would forget that this "company"
I worked for could not afford an office, that it rescinded on
health insurance and rarely delivered what it promised to me
or the clients. I simply chose to believe there would be a happy
ending to this story, as my boss liked to purport ad nauseum.

On the other hand, I was secretly thrilled that this job
entailed only a weekly meeting in a coffee shop, that I could
work at home, and that I could keep my own hours, and since
the company had little business, I managed to get all the work
done and still have plenty of time on my hands.

After my meeting with her, I went home and called the
owner of an underfunded golf destination club, about an internet ad, which I was writing to save our company money. Then
I called an underfunded real estate company in New Mexico
about a press release, which I was writing to save our company
even more money. I checked my emails and then I looked out
my window at a sunny day on Second Avenue, people walking
slowly in the warmth, girls in very short skirts and men with
swivel heads on cellphones.

I called Arieh. I called him because here we were, both on
the same planet in the same year in the same city on the same

sunny day—a miracle of a sort. I asked him, "What are you doing?"

"Working."

"I thought I'd come over this afternoon."

"Come over then," he said simply, as if A equals B. He could as easily have given one of his other standard replies, "Why would I want you to come over?" But this time he didn't, so around 2 pm, I took a cab again (I had every intention of taking the bus but it's as if my anxieties run on taxi time) and Arieh answered the door naked except for blue underpants, sighed dramatically and shook his head as he let me in.

Translated: You again. Why do I bother?

Or translated in Yiddish: I'm happy to see you.

I wasn't sure.

Then he strode right back to his desk where he returned to reading a legal document pulled from the top of a very tall pile of legal documents.

"What did your father die of?" he suddenly asked me.

"I already told you," I said, "lung cancer."

What does that have to do with anything, I wondered. My father died years ago. But Arieh is obsessive with questions since he is a lawyer and apparently a good one, according to him, with the highest rating, even though he is without an office or secretary and lives with files everywhere, on the floor, his conference table, his desk. How can he be a good lawyer?

And I regret to say a part of me admired this working of his against the grain. I even believed that he was a good lawyer. Certainly he was aggressive and anal retentive enough. Why would he need a conventional office, I thought? For that matter, why would I?

I went past him to the bedroom, lay down and pulled "Ecclesiastes" out of my bag, which I was reading at his suggestion. I heard him call out to me, amid his phone calls, "What are you doing?"

The first time I did not answer, because I knew it would only be moments before he would come in to check up on me to make sure I was not doing anything that would annoy him, such as putting a glass on his wooden side table, or taking a book out of his bookcase and not putting it back properly. This when the room looked like it had been hurled to and from Kansas.

It was amazing to me, that in as much disarray as this apartment was, his closets, however, were filled with very expensive suits (his "thin" suits—he couldn't wear them now) and ties organized methodically and fastidiously, all hanging carefully and perfectly, as if he were Brooks Brothers.

My mother had the same idiosyncrasy. She left my father and me when I was four. Later, when I tried to get to know her, I was struck by her strange obsession with neatness. She also had an impeccable, overflowing closet of orderly clothes. And she, just like Arieh, had the ability to flail her moods around with abstract expressionist intensity.

The second time Arieh called out to me from his desk, I answered, "Reading," and he immediately burst into the bedroom, an enormous stomach preceding him. Without his extra 60 pounds, he would be a handsome man.

"Very professional outfit you wear to your office," I said, gazing at his tiny blue underpants.

He replied, "What do I care? My life is over, and you are part of the reason, you and your dishonesties."

I pulled him to me. That was my life strategy then: Believe these long shot horses would come in, despite all evidence to the contrary. No wonder my company hired me.

He smiled at me and said, "Do you want to fuck?"

"Okay," I said.

He pulled his underpants down and I wondered, as I always did, if I would be able to breathe when he was on top of me. I took off my skirt and tube top and we did fuck, or make love, what's the difference, quickly, because he had work to do and so did I and then he went back to sitting in front of his computer and his tower of legal documents.

I left the apartment saying, "See you," before he could get a chance to spit out any of the usual frogs that jumped out of his mouth: How evil I am, how inhuman, and I began to walk the twenty blocks home in the warm and golden sun. No cab, it was so beautiful out.

My cellphone rang as I was walking down Second Avenue.

"That girl you sent to help me with my filing system, what was her name?"

"Claudia."

"Yes, Claudia," Arieh said, "she was completely useless. She misfiled two folders and constantly wrote down court dates without writing down which court. I told her repeatedly."

"I'm sorry. I didn't know she was stupid," I said, trying to hear him over the trucks and buses.

"It's impossible," he said. "I'm exhausted. Nobody can do this alone. I should have a huge law firm by now."

I had heard all this so many times before, that I just changed the subject. "Did you know that Annie keeps referring to visiting a friend in the hospital as a mikveh?" I laughed because the right word is mitzvah which means good deed and her word, "mikvah", means ritual bath. I am proud to say that, unlike Annie, I know the difference, mostly because he had taught me.

"That's priceless," he said, because he was absolutely rigorous about language and Judaism. They say that people who don't have feelings are often religious. I am interested in this and wonder what it means. That the rituals have the feelings for them? That unfeeling people understand an unfeeling God?

We hung up and I continued my walk.

I stopped, on my way home, to sit in St. George's Park on 2nd and 15th, a small park where mostly old people sit after getting their news from the hospital across the street, a gentle park full of huge trees and cobblestone paths reminiscent of London.

I was born in London and came over to North America as an infant but I feel I know London, even though it's mostly through my imagination. Thank you Virginia Woolf.

But sitting in the sun on that quiet afternoon with St. George's Park's trees in full regalia around me, I felt happy for a change. I felt a surge of love for this unkind, impossible man who has somehow torn, thus touched my heart.

I told myself that happiness is in the loving no matter what or who the object of my affection.

I could hear him retort, "No it isn't. We just have chemistry."

Chemistry? Chemistry for this enormous balding man with his wide buttocks, with a penis hidden under many folds? My life heretofore had been with athletic men, kind men, good men whom I seem to have found too dull or too suburban or not smart enough. Chemistry with someone whose intelligence mostly shone in the speed and abundance of ways he thought up to find fault with me?

As I was musing, a very tiny corgi puppy with snow-white markings and a caramel coat raced up to my legs. She was so young that she wasn't sure where her limbs went yet. She plunked herself down next to my feet, and cuddled up softly against my skin. I petted her and she, like all dogs, wanted to up the ante, so she stretched herself up and put her forelegs on my thighs, to garner more affection. I then decided to see what her owner was like, and so I looked up and there stood a man wearing a baseball cap and huge glasses, staring down fondly at her with a sad, dazed face.

"Her name's Georgia," he said, and yes he had just got her, and he let me pull her onto my lap. She settled in like a cat and I loved her and life at that moment. The sun, the dog, the trees in the park, words, great writing, music, friendship, Arieh who hurts me; and I thought, beauty, beauty, that's what means anything. That's all.

TWO

To that end, I decided to go to the seaside for the weekend but, when I actually thought it through, I was too poor to go. If I had a lot of money, I would get on a plane, rent a car and put myself in a hotel room with sliding glass windows that look out over that eternal motion. But I couldn't, even though I know how the sea restores my well-being.

My father and I often went to the sea together to distract ourselves from our being two emigrants marooned from normal family life. Years later, he told me we stayed in bed and breakfasts by the sea when I was a baby and he would leave the lights on when he went out drinking so I wouldn't be frightened, and he would return to a room infested with myriad black insects covering the lamps. He found this story amusing.

But we continued going to the sea together as I grew up, drinking and talking about the pleasures of a life that never bothered itself with the mundane considerations of financial security, the boring repetitions of family responsibilities, the constraints of a clung-to-career.

My little girlfriends were not allowed to spend time with me, their parents not admiring childhoods spent in bars, which, according to my father, made these children much the worse for it. So we were a solitary duo, my father and I.

Fortunately, once my mother left us, he was more interested in scotch than stepmothers. I was in agreement with this line of thinking. Let me be the sole woman in his life and therefore not be abandoned again.

The ocean was again my refuge in my twenties, after I left my father alone to his private sea of scotch, wine, cognac, green chartreuses and martinis. I went to the sea to mother myself, to soothe myself on the warmth and richness of beaches and sea roses and vistas of magical island light. This was where

I met my husband, a sailor. But even though we loved each other, we never managed to get on an even keel. He said I did not know how to bond. He told me I did not know how to accept love.

After my marriage ended, the sea was where I went again, this time for trysts. I didn't understand marriage, and to continue in this vein, it seemed what I mostly understood was the excitement and devastation of shipwrecks.

I had mentioned to Michael, a rich and cultivated man I knew, a man who was reasonable and kind and loving to me, if a little boring, that I felt like going to the coast for the weekend. He left me a message that he had reserved a car in case I wanted to go, even if I wanted to go by myself. Of course I wanted to go by myself.

Michael was always efficient and thoughtful. For some reason, I had no time for him.

It was right after I received Michael's message that Arieh called. He liked to call incessantly.

"How are you?" I asked.

"Bad," he answered. Standard reply.

"Why?"

"I looked at a new office," he said, "and the fresh paint made me ill. I had to come home and go to bed. I've been watching the movie, *David and Lisa*. And now, now I want to go and eat something."

"I have a conference call at 7 pm," I said.

"Let's go now," he said, "before your call."

He picked a Brazilian restaurant near us.

We walked in, the only two people in this enormous modern restaurant with shiny white tablecloths and mirrors on the ceiling and a black-and-white tiled floor, as if we had walked onto a Broadway dance number without any performers.

It was about 4.30 in the afternoon, too early for the other diners.

The waiter, a Brazilian, was short, quick, dark and handsome. He seemed to know Arieh. That was not surprising. Arieh has a passion for everything Brazilian. Antonio Carlos Jobim. The endless meat in the restaurants. The beaches and the Rio boardwalk. The mountains. The women's rear ends. He once told me that the first time he arrived in Rio, he sat down in the airport, frightened that the place would not live up to his dreams.

Apparently it did.

Apparently he came here a lot too.

The waiters started to circle us like buzzards, with an unending supply of legs of different kinds of meat—lamb, beef, pork—which they sliced off for you according to your nod. Right up his alley.

It was too early for me to eat, so I ordered a tea.

Arieh might have been ill, but he managed to eat two salads dripping in Roquefort, one overflowing vegetable plate and eight kinds of meat. I sat across from him, feeling I was out with Henry the Eighth. He also had his requisite glasses of red wine.

"I am rewarding myself for being ill," he explained.

Then he began talking. "Lisa in *David and Lisa* reminded me of you, proving you are mentally ill. I am too. We both are, after what we have lived through."

He meant unloving parents, parents who were unglued by the holocaust. His mother was taken to Auschwitz and watched her own terrified, starving mother walk her way to the gas chambers. Her father shot. Arieh's mother had her back broken at the whim of an SS officer, a gun put to her head—all of this when she was sixteen.

His mother, not unexpectedly, was not a good mother.

My mother's family was also sent to Auschwitz. She, however, escaped. To Haifa in Palestine, which is where, Arieh was born, after the war. We have this family history in common.

To go back to my mother, years later she escaped again, but this time from my father and me, as I've already said.

Obviously, she did not put much faith in happiness to be found in family ties.

Neither of our mothers did, not Arieh's, not mine.

And we, ourselves, hadn't either.

"It will happen again," he said.

He said this while I was thinking how the only place where Arieh was happy was a restaurant. He liked pontificating at a table. My British father was like that too, always in restaurants and bars. Arieh preferred eating to drinking but he, also, was always out.

Even I know it is a way to avoid intimacy. I have the same inclination.

"What will happen again?" I asked.

"They'll kill all the Jews," he said.

"What do you mean? In the States? They're going to round up all the Jews?"

"Yes," he answered.

I replied, "The Jews own Hollywood and the financial district."

"Oh and the Czar didn't own anything?"

"Oh stop it," I said. "We live better than most people. We have lived over fifty years with food and apartments and jobs and freedoms. Stop it."

The waiter returned with yet another side of some animal. Arieh picked off two slices.

"Dr. Leli says I am like an orchid," he said. A strange image for this enormous man.

"Meaning what? You're a hot house flower?"

"No, I need a lot of being taken care of."

"That is true," I said. "That is true. I don't as much as you, but I do too."

"You need," he said, "oceans of it. Caring, and loving, and nurturing."

"Well, for that matter, everyone does," I replied.

"Not everyone," he countered. He always counters.

"Yes, everyone." I always counter too.

Then he began asking me if I knew the etymology of *Midrash*. Of *Mishnah*.

"Why do you insist that I learn all this Hebrew?"

"I am giving you something I care about."

I was trying to think what it was about this man that I loved so much. He was like a bullying child who wanted me to play with his toys and if I didn't he ended up throwing them at me.

That's why I found myself picking at some of his lamb slices, and some of his Brazilian salad, when I didn't want to. Nerves.

"You know," I said, "the kabbalah believes if you change your name, you can change your fate a bit. My ex-husband's aunt believed the same thing. She wanted me to change my name."

"To what?"

"To Jacqueline. His last name was Olson. So my ex said, I would have been Jackie O."

"I didn't know your ex-husband had a sense of humour."

"He had a wonderful sense of humour. Also he understood me. Once we were standing on a beach looking out at the sea and he pointed to a trawler and said, 'See the outspread wings of the mast where the fishing nets hang?' 'Yes,' I said. 'Those are called birds,' he said, and he just knew I would love that."

Arieh made no comment and began explaining to me how the boardwalk of Tel Aviv is identical to that of Rio's.

We carried on in this non sequitur way, which is the way of people who live in restaurants.

Finally, I said, "I have to go for my conference call."

He looked longingly at his second glass of wine, which was still unfinished.

"You can leave it," I said. "You can leave some wine in a glass. You won't die."

"You're right. You're quite the yidner."

I didn't know the word, but I could figure out it was something to do with being a nag.

On the street I said, "That is one of the definitions of an alcoholic. They can't leave an unfinished glass."

He said, "It's not that. It's the money."

I thought: same difference.

We were on Park Avenue and the sun ebbing in the early evening was a bit Brazilian itself, I thought, in its brightness and languor. People were leaving work and I grabbed a cab (Arieh snorted as he got in, "It must be nice to be rich," which I ignored in more ways than one) and dropped him off at Barnes and Noble in Union Square where he wanted to buy a DVD.

"Films are enormously important to me," he said, "because I have had a hard life and like to escape."

This child. This aching child.

After Arieh left me to go in search of some film into which he could escape, Michael called to say he was having dinner with a friend. He called me because he is used to being married and telling a woman his every whereabout. He would like me to be that kind of woman, one who cares about his every move and I wish I could.

"Have a nice time," I said, meaning it.

Go, go, I thought, to sane people, wherever they are.

Michael was a decent man and I wished I could spend my life having a predictable, nurtured life with him but I couldn't get away from the other one who seemed to be lodged inside me like a dybbuk.

.

THREE

The next morning, I put on exercise clothes and stopped off at the cleaners where the pretty Chinese girl who works there had a riveted audience in a man whose eyes followed her every move, as he picked up bags of clothes from the floor to take to the cleaning plant. She was delicate and smooth, as I once was, and I stared at her glowing skin and confident dark eyes, embarrassed at having somehow misplaced that part of myself.

She handed me my receipts, handed them over to this older woman that I am, and I smiled, sadly, that no more would men pop into where I was working just to feel the gaiety of female beauty, no more would a man stare at me while he was supposed to be getting on with his work.

I kept walking after I left the cleaners, on a beautiful summer morning, a quiet day, in a holiday week, July Fourth, and stopped off at the diner where I always go for two coffees, one for me and one for the man who trains me at the gym. I have a trainer, even though of course I can't afford one, but left to my own devices, I might confuse exercising with brushing up against machines.

I leaned into the Formica counter, while the dark urbane young waiter with a patrician, aquiline face, who always served me when I came for breakfast, was busy pouring my coffees. It was so beautiful out and he was so beautiful in here that I decided to be friendlier than I usually am.

"Where are you from?" I asked him.

That's what men used to ask me when I was younger, when I stood at counters waiting for coffees or stood in line at the bank. "Where are you from?" they'd ask.

Now I'm doing it.

"Cairo," he told me, "I was just back there two months ago."

Cairo. I had always wanted to live there; specifically I had always wanted to live in *The Alexandria Quartet*. When the four books ended, I didn't want to leave my Egyptian family of Clea and Nassim.

"Lovely," I said.

"We should go sometime," he said, teasing.

"You could fix me up with your grandfather," I replied.

He laughed.

I left the coffee shop thinking maybe that wouldn't be such a bad life, his tall mannerly grandfather and me sitting in the Egyptian sun, and then I wondered what's happened to the world so that now I am frightened to go to Egypt alone although the Arabs are so elegant and beautiful? Now, I conjure up pictures of beheaded journalists and crowds hating Westerners on principle and what world is this, such longing for Egypt, Tel Aviv, Damascus, Alexandria?

Once I got to the gym, I locked my money and lipstick in the gray boarding school lockers and went to the pull-up machine for my legs, lifted my tired old sawhorses and was appalled at the face grimacing across from me in the gym mirror. My face didn't at all reflect the young girl yearning and clamoring inside me.

The trainer arrived and immediately told me he was moving to South Beach because he had not found love here. He is Spanish and wants a beautiful "white girl" but he did not want to accept that New York girls want men who can help them with money and that an itinerant trainer of 40, living in a single room, is not what they want. Yet here I was myself, chasing after a man who himself lives in one messy room and has not even civility to offer me, while I chase, chase, so why was I ascribing survival traits I myself didn't have to all these other New York women?

The trainer told me he was reading a book on manners, always so busy he was, gauging the impression he made. He told me that someone had asked him to model, and he was doing a photoshoot next week. Him with his big muscles that should not be, as he explained to me, too big anymore. What people want, he said, is sleekness.

Later in the morning, my phone rang.

"Listen," Arieh said. "I can't do this. I can't forgive you. You have to live with what you did. I have to live with what I did. I cannot ever forgive you. I don't want to be reminded of all this every time I see you so we cannot go on. It's over."

I said nothing because already the terrible hurt was moving inside me. And then he hung up on me.

FOUR

I don't usually eat pizza but I love it. Pizza reminds me of men. Eating pizza is what you do in a normal relationship, not on a "date" where they take you somewhere fancy. When you belong to a man, you just get a piece of pizza and sit down together.

There's an older man in the neighborhood, a Spanish guy, Joey, who comes in to help me when things go wrong in my apartment, such as a fuse breaking or my phone going on the blink. We've become friends over the years and now he often just drops by to chat. He brings me little gifts, a jazz CD he's found, once even a ring he picked up on the street, which he was sure, was a diamond and I was sure it was not, and unfortunately I was the one proved right. He has even left money on the table for me. Just because, he says, "Someone has to watch out for you."

The day after Arieh ended it, Joey stopped by because now he was on chemo and had the "blahs," he said.

"Not the blues?" I asked.

"I wish I had the blues," he said, sitting primly on my piano bench. I looked over at his closely cropped gray hair, his piercing black eyes and felt such affection.

This guy was a killer with women when he was young.

I told him I had the blues and how Arieh had just ended it with me. I have told Joey this story many times before, of Arieh ending it, and every time I have told it, I have been lying down on my couch. "It's him," Joey said. "Not you. It's his problem."

Everyone was saying that.

Or maybe I was finally hearing it.

"Let's get some pizza," he said, "across the street." It was about 5 o'clock and the summer light was getting soft and there was a slight breeze as if we were sailing so I got up off the couch and went with him, just for the ordinariness of it. I ordered a mushroom slice and he chose pesto and cheese and we sat outside on plastic green chairs and watched the people attached to backpacks and on cellphones walking their dogs.

Joey was tired from the chemo but in good spirits. He told me his colon cancer is an "elixir" for him.

"An elixir?" I repeated.

"Yeah," he said in his bass voice. "That's because death, which I've flirted with for so long, finally knocked on my door."

"You're not dying," I said, but I was only too aware that when you are about to lose something, it can take on unendurable beauty.

"No, but I've always been thinking about it," he answered.

Then he told me his first wife is trying to get back with him. She knows the complete schedule of his chemo.

"I don't blame her," I said.

He laughed. "You couldn't be with anyone. You're too much like me. A dog."

If only, I thought.

I held my cellphone closely in case Arieh called.

That's when the 2nd movement of Ravel's *Piano Concerto in G* that I have chosen as a cellphone ring started playing.

"Hello," I said a bit desperately, only to feel immediately annoyed. It was Michael, the nice man. "I'll call you back," I said. "I am sitting here with Joey."

It was dawning on me that if I did nothing, just held on and didn't get so anxious that I brought all the curtains down on myself, life continued. Pizzas and phone calls and kindnesses and scat jazz that I just had to let happen. Be passionate about your passions, a friend said. And pizza and Joey and the nice man were not my passions but they weren't in the way of them.

While I was sitting out there, my cellphone rang again. I looked at the number, still hoping it was Arieh, but it was an old lover, David, with his Don Johnson sunniness. He wanted to let me know that a scheduled golf game he had with my best friend needed to be rearranged. "You'll be talking to her, no doubt," he said. He never paid much attention to arrangements, but over a golf game, he was Johnny on the spot.

This is normal life, I thought. People playing golf (which I don't. I go with friends to their club and lie by the pool trying to make sense of Spinoza and they return, one talking louder than the other, Did you see my swing?) Those kinds of afternoons in the sun had a bonhomie that, in my continual twisted desire for Arieh; I was no longer a part of. My ex lover David did not know this.

"I'll buy you a new record player," David added, once we had gone over the changes in his plans. He broke my record player a long time ago.

He has a girlfriend now and doesn't realize that connecting with me could hurt me, especially when I was this vulnerable. But I said, "Okay," knowing he was a man of grandiose promises. He wouldn't get me a new record player because he was never around. Joey would be the one to fix my record player, although I wouldn't be able to figure out how to play it.

Joey attached a DVD player to my TV but it turns out I need to be drunk to know how to work it.

"I would have thought you would have ten new boyfriends by now," David said to me, on the phone.

"Not when you're 57," I said. "Any ideas on how to attract them?"

"Stand around and smile," he said.

David and I speak about twice a week. For 20 years we have been in touch. For ten of those years, he was in prison for growing marijuana and I was married. He used to call then. When he got out I was not married and we had an affair but I would not let him move in with me. I wasn't ready and he wasn't either, or at least I told myself that. Thus I arranged it that we were once again relegated to the phone. Finally he got a girlfriend. We're still on the phone.

After the pizza, I went home to lie down on my couch and read about the Kabbalah. I read about mental journeys where you make contact with angels who tell you about your life and your destiny. I read a story by a Hassidic rabbi, an old legend, where God says that giving your life for another or having a baby are not the highest good that a human can experience. What is? the angel asks God. And God answers, through a parable, of course, that the highest good is, let me note this, forgiveness.

My phone rang. It was Michael, constant as ever.

"No, I don't need the car to go to the seacoast," I said, "but thank you."

"Alright," he said. "Why don't you take a cab to Central Park and we'll take a walk?"

I thought, "Why not?" and, naturally, I took a cab, as he suggested. This one, for a change, was free because he gives me taxi money—he was always trying to entice me with his money which half impressed and half repelled me—and there he was waiting, seated on a stone bench outside the Park, wearing his boyish cap and unattractive beige windbreaker and brown wing-tip shoes. He stood up and we immediately began to walk quickly, for he is that kind of man, 'round the reservoir.

As we trudged along the gravel path, we both remarked on the almost spiritual silver stillness of the reservoir and the tall buildings gold in the setting sun round the park, elegant and majestic. We kept on walking as the light faded and the joggers lugged past us, over and over, and he began telling me he might do some real estate in South America, but then again he might not.

I told him that a life where he is sometimes in South America and sometimes in New York sounded pretty idyllic to me.

He looked at me. Idyllic enough to be part of? his eyes asked.

In novels, the heroine would marry this steady man and be bored out of her mind but at least be living a decent life. She would be bedeviled by thoughts of loving Arieh and go see a shrink who would tell her to leave the loving, civilized man . . . for him, the shrink.

That's what would happen in a story. But what happens in real life, I wondered, as we walked along.

We decided to have dinner. I didn't want to sit outside, just in case Arieh saw us. Arieh had a way of popping up in places. He had a way of referring in conversation to things I was thinking. I used to wonder if he tapped my phone.

So I said to Michael, as we passed the old New York mansion that was transformed into a museum of art, the Neue

Galerie, "Let's go in here." I didn't like being visible on the street with him.

And there we were in the Cafe Sabarsky, sitting at a little marble table with dark paneling round us; Viennese Sacher tortes, and strudels calling out to us, with a view of 5th Avenue and the Park. We were in Vienna in other words, and Michael asked me, "Why don't you have any relatives in Vienna?" meaning on my mother's side and I shook my head, infuriated, because Arieh, angry Arieh, he knows, he knows why I don't have relatives in Vienna, and this nice man, how the hell can he NOT know, is he not paying attention to this century, to the hurt infused throughout our literature? Is he not paying attention to anything, such as the agony I have been living in over the past year loving Arieh, in spite of or because of the dark forces that are brutally lodged in him, and I answered, so Michael could learn what is dangerous in life, "Hitler is the reason I don't have any relatives in Vienna."

And Michael nodded, distantly.

I let it go, thanks to a rather dry Gruner Veltliner I was sipping. This man is impervious, I said to myself, eating his palatschinken on a quiet Friday night in the city, two blocks from his large, rather pretty apartment that I refuse to move into, even though being on the Upper East Side with the park and the beautiful buildings and Michael's even temper could make me feel that I was beginning life again, in another city, this city of his, this city of well being.

But I didn't want it. I wanted the other one, the other one of Hebrew lessons and rage. I wanted the Arieh of wry laughter, humorous questions and intrusive assertions.

Just at that point, my cellphone began ringing insistently. I didn't answer it. I knew who it was because of its insistence. Why was he calling? To say something awful to me? Probably. Or maybe he missed me as much as I missed him.

I went home with Michael, cheerier, since some contact was made with my soul, Arieh reached out to it, and I tried to be kind to Michael for being so good to me, for not abandoning me, but I couldn't, and I took a taxi home (I didn't have the strength for the subway or a bus), and I noticed, once I got home, that my bed was unbearably hard and hurtful.

Friends who stay with me always comment on it. "You need a new bed," they'd say. But I never paid much attention to it. I had been sleeping in an uncomfortable bed for over ten years. So what?

But now I was feeling it.

Maybe Joey would help me buy a new one, I thought. He likes to shop.

One could say that I was ready to do something tangible.

FIVE

I woke thinking about people who live without love and only have work. People absolutely riven with passion. Nietzsche. Beethoven. But those were geniuses and maybe the fire of their work sustained them. Although, I doubted it. In the case of Ludwig, it was his anger that kept people away. The pressure, the pressure, I suppose, of his work was so powerful that he could not get on with anyone. Or maybe his mind moved so much more particularly.

I could not give myself such a lofty excuse.

I called Joey, before I even got up.

"Want to help me buy a bed?" I asked.

"Only if I can try it out with you."

"Don't give me that Spanish flirt stuff. Just come with me. I hate buying practical things."

"You're not kidding."

"I told Michael about needing a new bed and he suggested some kind of under mattress thing, a temporary solution, to make it softer."

"Just buy the damn bed. That sounds too crazy."

"It does, doesn't it? It's too fucking measured," I said, looking for ammunition against Michael. Ah, that's why I don't love him. He believes in mattress enhancers, not an actual bed.

"I'll start looking for you. There's some cheap places around here," he said.

"I could probably do it on the internet," I said.

"Just let me look," he said.

"Okay. Don't look hard. Only if you're near a bed store. I can go later myself," I said.

"You'll never go."

"You never know," I said. "I'll call you later," and hung up feeling some game, although I was not sure what, was afoot.

I put the phone down and then went back to that horrible preoccupation of noticing that Arieh had not called back. There was no call either when I went out to breakfast at an outdoor Polish cafe that he and I used to go to. A restaurant I used to feel happy in, with him, as we spent mornings telling each other the names of streets from our childhoods or gossiped about people we knew, having long discussions with the leaves falling on our hair, the sun lighting our cheeks for just a few moments through the lattice of interlocking trees and canopies. The same restaurant where he once threw a glass of water at me. That was the day I told him that I was choosing Michael, just because Michael had been kinder to me. A month later, I tried to take it back.

As I sat alone with my fruit salad and coffee, I was surrounded by couples also sharing their morning. Some didn't talk to each other, reading the paper. Others shared banalities. I suppose there was love in these banalities and I envied them that, but maybe they looked at me and thought, Ah she is alone and can read the paper in quiet and she has the possibility of wonderful things happening to her because she is alone. Hah.

The next night, I went to see Michael again, to see if maybe I could love him, but as the evening eked along, my eyes kept going to his DVD digital clock. All I wanted was to get away. I felt distant as we sat on his uncomfortable couch covered with a rough green cloth, and he brought up the idea of my moving in with him.

However, I admired his diligence in trying to make us a couple. He said things like, "Did I tell you how much I love you?" "Did I tell you how beautiful you are?" "Do you need any money?" "Would you like to go somewhere warm for a holiday?"

It was strange that these were all questions. As if his feelings were tentative or as if he was pretending that he was not really trying to force a mountain to jump. Still, no one had ever been as considerate of me as Michael was.

He also said he would move his bookcases into the other room, and then I could move my bookcases into this room, he would buy me a desk and a computer, and I thought No, No, this conversation is supposed to be giggly, happy, an overflowing of hope together. Not feeling like I am about to be locked up in a box.

Michael believed that if you enact the right conventions, take appropriate actions, these will forge a relationship. For all

I knew he was right. He believed if you take steps toward commitment, you arrive at commitment.

I wish I were capable of committing to such a thought.

But my commitment was to something else. I just wasn't sure what it was. This something that I was committed to lay insistently and mysteriously underneath my obsession and grief over Arieh.

So, as always, I left Michael's apartment early, feigning tiredness or something equally anemic, and took a cab home, even though I was getting near to no money, but I was too weak, I told myself, to take public transportation, so weak from Arieh not being in contact with me. Then I remembered Arieh didn't call me on Christmas either or on New Year's or Passover or Rosh Hashanah. He did not wonder if I was alone and hurting as he abandoned me for my sin of having, at one time, abandoned him. He did not wonder if that particular loneliness on those holidays would remind me of being alone and abandoned before.

Now he was silent and I was left with, dammit, my self. My uncomfortable bed. Perhaps I did not notice, in the past year, how hard my bed was because I was being treated so harshly in his soft bed.

SIX

I want to tell you how I got myself into this mess. By the time I finish this story, I may tell you how I got out of it. When you fall in love with a man who hurts you, or whom you hurt, clearly, you are reliving old hurts. Clearly you are trying to heal those old hurts by finally feeling them. They need reckoning with.

Those old hurts insist on it.

And so, some hurtful situation comes along for you to fasten yourself onto so as to clear the whole mess up. The past, the present, and the future.

The chaos, in other words, gives birth to a new self. For him and for you.

But none of it, none of it goes as you expect it to.

One August evening, almost three years before I began this tale, I stepped out of a cab on West End Avenue, over the Hudson River, just as the sun was getting a bit soft and sultry. I raced across the street in scuffed gold mules and a silk black dress. I had a red sweater wrapped round my shoulders and I was carrying a book. My hair flew around my shoulders as I ran and I was trying to simultaneously gauge the traffic and the crowd of people waiting for me in the small park at 79th and West End. They were friends of Joanne's and I didn't know them, but it was better than being alone with Joanne, since that can be too intense, too many questions about my life, not that I mind the questions, I just didn't have any answers.

Everyone was quickly introduced, two men alone, another man and his wife and new baby. We all began walking to a bar near the water. Arieh, whom you know about, who was not fat then, just tall, was studying me and began asking me where I was from, where did I live, what did I do. He seemed to annex himself to me, look down at me with great curiosity. He moved near me and talked about Montreal where I grew up.

"The French Canadians are anti-Semitic, aren't they?" he asked as an opening gambit.

"No," I said, "they were an oppressed culture, too." But I didn't know. Before knowing him, I did not spend all my time thinking about the plight of the Jews.

He began speaking in French, better than mine. That's because he has a flair for language. He is like a monkey or parrot. He picks up the sound instantly. Language is easy for him. Just not life.

He asked me what I was reading. I showed him *Sepharad*. "Ah Spanish for Sephardic," he said. I had been wondering what it meant. He went on to talk about Sephardic Jews and I listened, while watching the sun sinking into the river, and the water turning golden and New York wide and open in the evening, feeling rather held by the beauty of the night and the sound of this man's articulate milk chocolate voice. It was a rare conversation and that struck me. Most men seemed to lag behind in discussion.

We walked and I wondered if Joanne liked him. I thought he was a sort of date for her. He seemed pleasant enough, I thought, but Joanne, at 56, financially secure, and impatient, doesn't usually like any man that much. I slowed down my pace so Arieh could catch up to Joanne, and I moved myself to talk with the other single man in the party, Ron, who told me about his upcoming divorce and how he was worried about his daughters. I thought that his worrying about his daughters was really his worrying about himself.

Occasionally both men would break into Hebrew. "Ah you're both from Israel?" I asked curiously.

Ron, the divorcing man, said, "What of it?"

I was struck by the aggressiveness of his answer. "Just asking."

They were both Israelis, both Americanized. Ron was a successful software company owner who had sold out, gotten rich, and was now studying Jewish theology. Arieh, the man I was to lose my heart to, or was it my mind, was a lawyer who obviously had a penchant for talking, for books, for words.

I had once freelanced on a paper about daughters and fathers so this was why I was listening to the divorcing man drone on and on about his family situation. I sensed I wasn't getting the real story. He made sure to mention that his wife was crazy. She didn't used to be, he said, but she became that way. They all say that. And they all act like they had nothing to do with it.

Arieh and I went up to the bar to get everyone drinks. I hated the music. "Why don't they just stop?" I said to him. He made no comment. Obviously bad rock didn't drive him to illness as it does me. I wasn't sure I could stay and listen to this flat, out-of-tune singing.

The bar only took cash.

"I don't have any," he said, looking at his credit cards.

"I have a lot," I said. "I just went to the machine." I have a child's attitude to money. Here is a handful, let's spend it.

He said, "I'll send you a check."

I laughed.

"No need," I said.

He danced awkwardly with Joanne to the bad music and Ron told me more about his divorce.

We all decided to have dinner together.

"You sit here," Arieh said to me in the restaurant when the group of us gathered round a table. He pointed to the seat next to him. At first, for a woman, this is seductive, a man inserting himself into your life, this taking of her.

I began talking with the new mother on my left about her relationship with the baby's father whom she was not married to but who was crazy about this new child. The father was a womanizer and I wondered how women go mad for the oddest men, this unprepossessing, not particularly interesting LA lawyer.

God knows I would soon learn how easy it is to go mad for the oddest men.

Joanne talked to Arieh and Ron, and, finally, politics came up and Arieh turned and asked me about my views and I said, teasingly, "I'm an anarchist."

He said, "Oh really?"

I knew he interpreted the word as it was meant to be: politically.

"What do you mean?" he asked.

"The way I live my life. I like the idea of no rules."

I could tell he thought I was an idiot. Anarchists meant something to him. He could place them in history. Like a good Jew, he believes one has to take a pre-emptive stand. He knew what came of not taking stands. He probably hated anarchists, but, being anarchistic, I didn't care.

"What do YOU believe in?" I asked. Just to get off the subject.

"In love," he replied.

I smiled and moved my eyes toward Joanne, "And how is it going?"

"I don't know." He turned to me, "I've only just met you."

I went for it, like a newborn for the breast.

SEVEN

Four days later I received a check from Arieh for $40 with no note attached. I told my friend Marsha about it. I said, "It's a sign. It's a sign I am no longer attractive to men. It changes after fifty."

I called Joanne, through whom I had met Arieh, to tell her. "He's very nice. He did the gentlemanly thing of sending me the money I paid at the bar."

"Strange he doesn't carry any cash on him," Joanne said.

That Friday night I was home alone, a little bored, a little lonely, about to settle in and read a book. How had my life come to this? I used to have a boyfriend around.

The phone rang. "Did you get my check?"

"Yes thank you. Why didn't you send a note?"

"I'm ashamed of my handwriting."

That was an odd response, I thought. I, myself, have terrible handwriting and, of the many things I am ashamed of, that is not one of them.

"You could have typed a note," I said, which is what I would have done.

"Yes a friend of mine said I should have sent a note."

That was intriguing to me too. He had been talking to someone about this exchange. It mattered to him. It wasn't just mailing off a check.

I regret to say my vanity raised its energetic, ever-ready, little head.

Then he added, "I rushed home every night expecting you to call. But you didn't."

Why did he think I would call him, I wondered. It had never even occurred to me to do so.

"What are you doing now?" he asked.

"Nothing."

"Want to have dinner?"

"Okay."

And he raced down, he only lives 20 blocks away which in New York is a neighbour, one mile, and I came downstairs and it was another warm summer night and we went to a corner bistro and sat outside. We both liked to be outside, and he told me about the cafes in Israel, how everyone sat outside, and these outdoor cafes in my lively bohemian neighborhood reminded him of Israel, where he had been happy.

He was born in Haifa, which was where my own mother had escaped to from Vienna. He told me that Austrian and German Jews were called *yekkes* there, people who had clocks instead of hearts, were "just so." I hadn't known this and found it amusing. I did have a bit of that trait, since I am never ever late for anything, and then we walked some more, and he told me that his family left Israel when he was seven and it was the saddest thing, to leave that land of sun and beauty, and come to the States to massive dark crowded buildings in the Bronx where people made fun of him because he couldn't speak English.

We went for a nightcap at a Mexican place nearby.

"I have this terrible job," I told him. "I commute to Long Island, almost two hours each way, which is bad enough, but the company is being indicted, a documented ship of fools," I said. "I waste my time writing emails for them. I hate it."

He smiled and said, "No one should ever be on Long Island. There's something wrong with the place. I had to spend time there when I was in college and all I could think about was I was being infected by some strange perverse air of placidity and stupidity."

I liked that. Not all men hear you. They quickly return to their own performance piece. I felt rather alive with his attention because when I added that "Writers are like buggy whip makers now, they're passé," he nodded.

"You're right," he said.

Again, he seemed to understand what I was saying.

I felt free with him, and he kept correcting my grammar, "He and I," he'd say, "not he and me."

"It's funny," I said under a street lamp as I started to walk him part way home, "I don't mind that you do that. It's like your having perfect pitch."

At that he leant over and kissed me. I pulled back a bit. I am not, as you can tell, easy with intimacy, and it wasn't yet sexual between us, the sexuality was in the talking.

He stuck his tongue inside my mouth, pushed it in, but God knows he isn't the first man not to notice what a woman isn't feeling yet.

The next morning, he called early to say he wanted to come over. Again, my vain little head. He likes me, it said.

He arrived, sat on my couch, and proclaimed that he was very tired. It was only eleven in the morning.

Why was he here?

"I'm working," I said. "So take a nap."

Which, to my surprise, he did. He went into my bedroom and, to more of my amazement, undressed, leaving only his underwear on, and got into my bed. I shrugged my shoulders, slightly amused at this audacity and strange willingness to be intimate at such an early stage of our not knowing each other. Getting to know someone is always full of bizarre turnings. It feels strange. This is just another example, I told myself.

I turned and went to my office, and left him in my bed, resting. After about an hour, I went back into my bedroom.

My bedroom faces out over gentle trees, which is rare in New York. The light is soft.

I lay down beside him, because in a way I liked this insinuation of his. It seemed like courage, courage to get close,

I thought. And, since I am timid in love, someone being audacious can push things forward.

He held me and said, "I've done unspeakable things."

"We all have. Anyway nothing is that unspeakable," I said. "I have too. Like what? What could be so unspeakable?"

"I've been a cross dresser, gone to massage parlors, all kinds of things . . ."

I was shocked. A cross dresser? I had never met a cross dresser before. What does that mean?

"Are you gay?" I asked.

"No, it's just a way of being fragmented. A way to hate myself."

I studied him and stroked his thinning hair. This tall, balding man who is good with words.

His mother tortured in Auschwitz, his orphaned father in Siberia. Unspeakable things.

He dresses as a woman to be with his mother.

"I get it," I said, thinking out loud. "You want to be humiliated as she was in the camps. You want to join her. It's too cruel to leave her alone."

He focused his sad dark eyes at me intently through his glasses. His expression did not betray any emotion. Maybe just a quick wisp of surprise that I was trying to understand.

"Maybe," he said.

I was thinking about his confession and it seemed he was telling me, "Don't fall in love with me. I am ill."

At that moment, I said to myself, Saved. God knows what he's done. Yet, I admired that he was so honest. He was telling me the truth right off. He wasn't hiding his weaknesses, like most people do. That's something. As I said that to myself, I realized how lonely I was.

"Let's go out and have lunch," I said.

We sat in the sun and talked about trips he had taken. We both loved Lugano. I had a distant relative who lived there. He apparently had been there with some French girl who was just a friend. Something flickered in me at that moment. Few men my age travel with female friends, men don't really want female friends, they want to fuck, and then my mind switched to remembering my second great aunt in Lugano who had bought me dresses and told me stories, each day, of friends who had lost everything in the war and then regained themselves, usually by marrying a Swiss banker. I had loved my piano-playing aunt and her handsome elegant formal husband. They kept a candle in the window for the dead.

At lunch, Arieh told me how much he loved Rio, Paris, Barcelona, Haifa. He loved these cities more than anywhere. He loved to talk about being away, being somewhere else. He went on to describe the layout of the cities, various street corners. I thought he must not like the present that much.

Of course it came out he had no grandparents thanks to Hitler but of course I knew that. The longer we talked it became more clear that we were two Americanized children of European Jews.

He tucked his napkin into his shirt and, speaking Italian with the waitress, ordered a black pasta and a tricolore salad "serra formaggio." With this, he ordered a red wine from Sicily, and the fact that he did, that he insisted on having wine with the meal, plus his obvious love of cafes—reminded me of my childhood. It was familiar in a way that very little else in my life was.

My mother, too, made jokes, bitter jokes all the time when I saw her. We would meet in cafes and I would respond in kind, with my own irony, our mutual attempt at levity, what with her having left when I was an infant, what with her being dead to love and family after the Second World War and all its dead.

And here was Arieh, making jokes in spite of his mother breastfeeding him bitterness after losing her parents and youth in Auschwitz and the belief in anything sweet. What else was there to do?

In other words, Arieh and I sat there teasing and drinking in the sun with our respective unacknowledged desperations.

It turned out we even had the same autocratic fathers. I could see Arieh's in the forcefulness in which he put forth his ideas. And my father was there in me, with my obvious fearfulness with men, my inability to bond.

Arieh and I had these similarities. Here we were, both in our mid fifties, childless, he never having married and I only barely.

In the beginning, we'd lie in my bed and hold each other and he'd say, "Do you know what the top of Haifa is called?"

"No."

"Mount Carmel, which is where your mother must have lived because that's where all the Austrian and German Jews went. They were the ones who wore ties and jackets while the rest of Israel had their shirtsleeves rolled up. The filmmaker who made Shoah made a film called *Why Israel* and he interviewed the German Jews and he asked them 'What Did You Give Israel' and they said, 'Everything.'"

I'd lie silently next to him and remember my mother's all-knowingness. A Germanic trait?

"You would love Israel," he said, holding me tight. "People are just like you. They sit outside talking and joking and you could wear your sandals and dresses because it's so warm all the time. There is irony everywhere. And kindness. For instance, I was walking in Tel Aviv one day and I passed a woman walking, she was beautiful, Russian, her husband was still in jail in Russia, he was well known, and she was alone on Shabbos and crying and two old women begged me to walk her home, so she was not alone. This happens all the time."

Still? I wondered.

His tales interested me.

He was telling me of a family I could have belonged to.

My mother never once referred to her Jewishness. She prided herself on being an anti-Semite. But I wondered, How could she forsake her relatives who fared so badly? Her negation broke my heart. Of course, it did. I was also a relative and she had no problem forsaking me either.

So there I was listening, wanting to find my lost tribe.

That was on good days. Most days, however, he only had words for all the hurts he had experienced, betrayals by friends, girlfriends who slept with friends, clients who didn't pay him, parents who couldn't love him. He wailed. He was screaming at the sky about missed opportunities, the unfair loneliness of his life—all of which I felt about my own life, too, but didn't feel it appropriate to scream about. He went on and on. The pain of having parents who had been treated brutally and only knew how to be brutal themselves. A legacy of loss and unkindness. I knew all about that but I kept it more to myself. It fascinated me, this raging into the night. But what seas could he take me on?

"Do you love me?" he'd ask, as he walked me each night to my door after dinner. We'd find restaurants half way between our homes. I would be exact about the distance.

"That place is 10 1/2 blocks between," I'd say.

"A *yekketah*," he called me, which was the female of a *yekke*, a person with the heart of a clock. A person who is fastidious.

"Do you love me?" he'd ask.

"As far as I know you."

And then he'd just stand at my door. To prolong saying goodnight, he'd tell a joke. About the Pope meeting the Chief Rabbi. The Pope in his opulent vestibule has two phones, one of which is solid gold, and His Eminence tells the Rabbi that the solid gold phone is his Direct Line to God but unfortunately he can't let the Chief Rabbi make a call because such a long distance call is so expensive. The Chief Rabbi completely understands. But when the Pope visits the Rabbi's broken down home, and his two phones are black plastic, the Rabbi tells the Pope he CAN use his direct line to G-D. "For us," the Chief Rabbi says, "it is a local call."

I laughed, I who normally don't like jokes, but Arieh told them with flourish. "It's like with Begin," he continued. Then he began acting a scene out from the Knesset, "Everyone was talking at once, and Begin was fighting with someone who said, 'Why should you befriend these people?' and Begin said, 'And what should I do? Befriend you?'" which wasn't quite as funny as his previous joke but his passion for the absurd was, and Arieh was enjoying my fixed attention, bobbing his head and stuttering and embellishing, and I found listening to him outside my door was a lot like flying.

He had an unending fount of stories. Once I responded favorably, there were three more.

"It's fascinating," I said. "These stories about *les Juifs*."

"But you're a Jew," he said.

"But I wasn't raised as one."

"But who cares. You are by rabbinical law. It's carried through the mother."

I smiled. So I belong somewhere, I thought. Someone may claim me. Then I smiled forlornly. Who will claim me?

"What happened?" he asked, looking at my face.

"Nothing," I said, and then I said, "Sleep well," and kissed him on the cheek and turned to go upstairs. We didn't sleep together.

Instead, we'd run to meet each other for meals. One afternoon, standing on a corner in the sun looking for a restaurant, he said, "I will hurt you. It is what I do."

I didn't say anything and put my hand gently on his then almost flat stomach and rubbed it. He just needs kindness, I thought.

"I've got to go to Florida to see my parents. Want to come?" he asked at dinner.

"No, but I'll drive you to the airport."

I liked to be with him. It felt lively. There was always a comeback—one didn't feel alone. As we drove off from the garage where I kept my old car, he asked, "Why do you tip the garage guys so much money?"

"They need it."

"And you don't?"

"That's not how it works."

He looked over at me and said nothing.

He heard what I was intending: Let me heal myself with kindness.

His intention was to fight. He was a litigator.

He kissed me goodbye as he got out of the car at the airport, like a wife.

"I think I might get arrested," he said.

"Why?"

"You're only ten years old."

I thought he meant my vulnerability, my yearning.

But now I think maybe it was something he said to all women, but I, I thought he was SEEING me. Ah, the terrible blindness of the needy mirror.

I called him when I got lost on the way home from the airport. A wrong road from Kennedy. Even though he was a lawyer, he had once driven a cab. Like me, he had struggled hard to get by. Nothing had been given to us.

On the cellphone while he waited for his plane, he directed me back onto the right road to Manhattan.

"You're lost without me," he said.

He didn't tell me I was going to become even more lost with him.

EIGHT

"That's him?" my best friend, Annie, asked when I pointed him out crossing a street towards us. "You find HIM attractive?"

He did look a little like a disheveled bear, whose thinning head fur was standing up, waddling towards us in wire rim glasses. His t-shirt had food stains on it. He who was always quick to be critical of what I wore. "Why do you dress like a nun?" he'd ask about my black dress, black sweater, ignoring I often wore colors on other days.

He joined Annie and I on the street and gave her a beguiling baby smile, as we made our way, naturally, to a restaurant.

She is a talker, like him, so it was only moments before they were on a conversational rocket ship.

"Mira tells me you love films, like I do," he said, as we were seating ourselves in a coffee shop that looked French with its marble top tables and black chairs, but is run by Arabs. Arieh pointed out how the owners were using their hands as they talked, as Israelis do.

"My husband and I see everything," Annie said taking off her coat. "We're embarrassing. Films for children. Shoot 'em ups. You name it."

"Yes," I threw in, "and they're not trustworthy. They recommend the worst ones."

"That's not true. We just saw *Waiting for the Barbarians*, that Canadian film . . . I loved it."

"That film was the second act of *The Decline and Fall of the American Empire*," Arieh said. "Denis Arcand made it. Same characters, twenty years later . . ."

"Really?" she said.

"Did you notice that?" he said aggressively to me.

"No," I said. Although I should have. I had seen both films. But I don't keep up with movies, as they do. I like to avoid reality as much as the next person, but these two choose to get lost in celluloid.

I get lost in books.

Annie looked like she was enjoying herself, smiling and sitting up straight, flashing her lively blue eyes, pondering whatever director's name Arieh put forth. I was happy for that.

Annie is a Midwestern blonde and the perfect *shiksa*. I could see him furtively looking at her full breasts, her full buttocks as she raced over to get the waiter.

She sat back down, the waiter now attentively standing by, and they both ordered teas and continued on about Lubitsch.

She seemed interested.

Finally he looked at me.

"Nothing to say?" he asked.

"What do you think of Bellow's writing?" I asked.

He didn't miss a beat. "Clever. But no passion. He's the opposite of Henry Miller."

"What do you mean?"

"Miller's writing is clunky but every page is full of passion, energy. Bellow can write better but it's all in the head."

The Word coming down to us.

I nodded, secretly pleased at his quickness, and then said that Annie and I had an important engagement, we had to get our nails done.

He was pleasant about it. No argument. He liked quick get-aways. They both stood up and said how much they had enjoyed meeting each other although when she said, "I always hate when Maynard and her (Annie pointed to me) won't go to westerns."

Naturally, he replied, "Maynard and she."

I noticed that her skin color changed a bit. Annie is not a person who likes to be corrected.

On the way to the nail place, she said, "Let's just say you and I like different types."

"That's true. You like them with money. Why don't I ever catch that from you?"

"He's smart, this one, but certainly not attractive."

"No," I said, hiding that I did find him attractive. Inexplicably.

"Also," she said, "he is completely full of himself."

I laughed. "That he is, that he is."

I think she thought he was just an aberration that I would shortly recover from.

But quite the contrary was happening. I was getting in deeper. Every night, it became a habit that he and I talked to each other on the phone, just rambling.

One night, he read me his favorite short story, as I lay in my bed.

"It's *The First Seven Years*. You know it?" he asked.

"No," I said, switching the phone to the other ear.

"Want to hear it?"

"Okay."

He began reading. After about the second paragraph I could hear sniffling and his voice cracking, although he kept on reading very carefully, very clearly, and movingly. The story was about a survivor of Auschwitz who had lost everyone and had no home anymore and worked humbly as an assistant shoemaker in a small town. He falls in love with the shoemaker owner's daughter who is kind to him. So he vows to marry her. He knows he has nothing to offer her so he works hard for seven years to win the hand of the girl. Needless to say, she marries someone else.

At some paragraphs, Arieh had to stop reading, he was crying so hard. When he finished, I said, "It's beautiful," which it was but I was almost more moved by Arieh's response. There is something hopeful about a man being undone by literature.

At the time, I couldn't figure out why he was crying like this. Later, I realized, it was because the protagonist was doomed to a life of loss. No matter how hard he worked, he couldn't get the girl. He would never be good enough because he had lost too much in the war and was losing again.

The decks were stacked against him.

Arieh cried unceasingly as he read the story.

At dinner the next night, as he was talking about Israel, one of his favorite subjects, and he was going on and on about how the world is against Israelis, I ventured, "Palestinian children get killed too."

It is by defiance we are saved, says Ben Franklin.

But Ben Franklin doesn't mention that after the defiance, comes the punishment. Is it by punishment that we are saved?

This conversation about Israel and Palestine took place in the Mexican restaurant of our first date.

"What exactly do you mean by that?" he asked.

"The tanks," I said.

"The Israeli army taught us not to kill civilians. I should know. I was in it."

"But everyone knows the tanks kill civilians," I said.

"What tanks exactly?" he asked sarcastically.

He is a litigating lawyer. I could not win in an argument and he knew far more about politics than I did.

"You're ignorant," he said. "You and your democratic politics are what leads to fascism. Not taking a stand leads to the gas ovens. You're a Nazi."

"Oh really?" I said, shocked. He couldn't possibly think that. I didn't yet know he talked in hyperbole.

I became confused. What should I be paying attention to? That he thinks I'm a Nazi or that democratic politics leads to fascism? In its skewed way, I could see what he was saying.

And maybe the Palestinians just have great PR. They show kids with sticks fighting Israeli tanks. I didn't know. And it was in my nature to side with the victim.

It was of course in Arieh's nature, too. And the victims were clearly and eternally the Jews.

"I can't talk to you," he said. "I don't want to even know someone like you," and he got up and walked out of the restaurant. It was to be the first of hundreds of times when my eyes would follow his implacable back as he left me alone in a restaurant or standing on a street.

He didn't call me for the next two months.

When he did call, as if no time had passed, he said, "Let's take a drive in the country. I told my client I'd drop off some files. We'll go in your car."

There was something about us, as if we were two children destined to go on adventures. I agreed to this field trip and forgave our last spat. Maybe I did have something to do with the argument, I told myself. What do I really know about Israeli politics? And anyway it would be nice to go to the country.

We drove up to Connecticut on a Sunday morning and met his British upper class friend and client, Michael, and sat on Michael's elegant porch, looking out over his rolling lawn and huge trees. The three of us had wine and ham and cheese and talked about books and music and movies and I was rather impressed by Michael's manners and understatement in contrast to the lordliness of his large house.

I found myself enjoying being with them and on the way home I thought Michael seemed more my type, musical, soft spoken, a man of taste. Arieh, in his incessant hatred of people and ideologies, seemed wrong.

Arieh was always complaining. His left testicle hurt. His knee ached. He had headaches. Didn't I notice his skin color? How he sweated all the time? He was ill, he said.

"The headaches are from the new flat screen TV I bought," he said.

I said nothing as I maneuvered onto the highway back to New York City.

"You don't believe me?" he asked.

"I don't know," I said.

"You don't believe in illness, do you?" He was staring at me aggressively.

I smiled meekly at him. "I believe this focus on illness is not healthy."

"You're saying illness is imaginary?"

"I wonder," I replied. "Some people are attached to illness."

"Is that so? I have been ill most of my life and you are saying it's not real?"

What illnesses was he referring to? Physical? Mental? Self-destructiveness? I understood that particular illness well. But I didn't hold much truck with talking about it.

"I don't know," I said.

Obviously I wasn't hiding what I thought because he got out of the car and did not speak to me for another four months.

NINE

During those breaks of contact, I didn't miss him. In those days, I didn't think I had anything to do with his eruptions. I didn't spend my time studying his behavior or mine.

I was busy. Movies, friends, music, work, walks along the city streets. I lived a life of pleasant dinners with pleasant friends. I followed my impulses. I thought, This is how one is free.

I had other suitors who were easier to be with. I went dancing with them, or to movies, and these men didn't argue with me. They might not have been as cerebral, or as inexplicably passionate about their ideas, but they were gentler.

I did not seem to want more from anyone. I was, in my way, still recovering from a divorce that I knew I was responsible for. I had been married to a good man and I had thought, I must be alone. I did not know about the rare gift of someone's love.

I had no sense of reality. I lived in my own fantasies that soon new love and success would come to me. I was vague about what I wanted and even vaguer about how to achieve it. Just give me life, I said, and it will do all the work.

Thus, Arieh was not on my mind. And I don't think much else was either. Something was turned off inside me. I had squeezed my eyes shut as a child and never fully opened them again.

When Arieh finally called, though, I would always meet him. It was as if I wanted to know the next chapter in the story. At our next detente, we had dinner in a small falafel place and he told me that you don't tell someone who is ill that their illnesses are imaginary. He had lost his career to illness, he said, he'd lost women, he'd lost his vitality. It was an inhuman thing for me to say.

I apologized.

As we walked, he told me he was seeing another woman who was very nice and a lot thinner than I am. The new woman is very beautiful. She had picked him up at a movie.

I was hurt, mostly at the much thinner comment, and I am sure that was why he had to mention it, and I said, "Ah."

I left him at his apartment door.

He did not tell me he was having an operation on his shoulder the next day.

A friend told me and I called him.

"Why didn't you tell me?"

"Why should I?"

We spoke every now and then. He lived his life. I lived mine.

He would tell you, now, that all hell broke loose between us when I slept with Michael, his English client. But I am going to tell you that all hell broke loose long before that.

All hell broke loose when my equally as quixotic, equally as abandoning, mother died.

My mother lived in London with her boyfriend who took care of her. She had Alzheimer's. She had no idea who I was but that really wasn't much different from the years before she had Alzheimer's.

My mother had said to me when I was four, as if addressing an adult, "You have to understand that I don't want to be a mother. You'll be an adult longer than a child, so what difference does it make if I leave you? We'll be friends when you're older."

She left my father and me and went to live with a French journalist, and then she left him and she was alone with many lovers and then she lived with an American writer, and I saw her occasionally. We never became the friends she said we would. It never worked. She had hurt me too much with her turning away. I perceived her lack of interest in me as an aggressive desire to wound me.

And, as far I was concerned, she had succeeded in her Mephistophelian plan to destroy me. I had no child. I had no husband. I had no formal training. I had been born to a life of no attachments. I felt she threw me to that bitter wolf. And, like all children who want to please their mother, I let that bitter wolf claim me.

But when I was four I thought with the creative mind of a child, Okay, this is how I'm supposed to behave. I am supposed to accept this. Sophisticated children raise themselves and accept that their mothers don't want to be mothers.

My mother, my rare mother, is too interesting to spend her time wanting to care or love me. My mother is too interesting to be nice to me or visit me or remember my birthday or Christmas. My mother is too interesting and witty to be bothered knowing what school I go to, or when I am hurt. My mother expects me not to feel sad or confused or need caring for.

She is too special, too free, too much of her own woman to be bothered with a child. I can't blame her.

It would be a complete waste of time and incredibly boring to be bothered with me.

The similarities between her and Arieh whom I told everyone was so interesting and nobody could see what I was talking about, with Arieh who never concerned himself with how his behavior affected me, had not yet occurred to me.

She was in a coma the last two days before she died, and I had gone to England to say goodbye. I frequently visited her over the years, telling myself she may not have been a good mother but that's not an excuse for me to be a bad daughter.

She was lying downstairs in what used to be Alan's (her boyfriend) dining room but was now being used as a hospital room. She was skeletal. Her eyes were closed. She did not move, nor eat; she just seemed to laboriously draw one last breath, then another. Her doctor and Alan were on a death-watch. We wet her lips. They told me that maybe she could hear. Alan stood tall and quiet, and said sadly, "Say something nice to her."

I couldn't think what to say. So I stroked her head and sat down in a chair near her bed and leaned in shyly toward her ear and said, "Such a pretty girl."

Which she had been and loved being.

Alan hovered about protectively. A doctor came back to the house and said, "It's only a matter of hours."

She died an hour after I spoke with her, just as I was in a cab on my way to catch a plane back to the States. It was in the days when I still had work commitments.

Alan called me as I was in the cab. "She's gone," he said.

"I'm sorry, Alan," I said. "You were so good to her. I'll come back next week for the funeral and help you clear things out."

I clicked the phone shut. I gazed dully out at the London traffic.

At the airport gate, I suddenly began to cry. My mother is dead, I thought, my mother. My mother who had not wanted to mother me but my mother.

On the plane I kicked off my boots and already I was missing her. She had been my adversary, been the model I had compared myself to for so many years. Her wit. Her looks. Her career. All of which seemed to eclipse mine.

Even her choice in men had been better. Her boyfriend was upper class English, Oxford educated, a famous screenwriter. They had had an affair for forty years while he had been married. When his wife died, and they were both seventy, Alan went to Montreal to move her to England to be with him. She was just starting to repeat the same questions twelve times, just starting to speak in monosyllables, just starting to get lost when she went out. She was, in other words, just starting Alzheimer's and he took care of her for the next ten years, as she lost language, continence, movement and comprehension, as if she was the most rare and valuable of offerings.

When I took them out to dinner and she would use her fingers instead of cutlery, and stare fixedly into nothingness, she who had been so quick with words, I would, to make conversation, ask him, "Well what was it like when you met her?"

And suddenly, he would light up and look over at her like she was thirty and breathtaking. "It was wonderful, wasn't it, Daisy?" he said to her.

She smiled, but she smiled like a baby does, at a wall.

I saw that he loved her with the same intensity he had in the first months he met her.

Two days after she died, in New York, my phone rang. I was sitting at my desk, looking out the window, wondering if the rain we were having had been sent from England to remind me.

"I heard about your mother." It was Arieh, of course.

"Yes."

"I'm sorry."

"Thank you."

We made banal chit chat and then got off the phone.

That night I had dinner with a literary agent friend, the type of man I should have been able to be involved with, an intelligent witty kind man, but no, no, he was too conventional for me. I can't live a normal life with a normal man, with pleasant dinners and gentle conversation. I need something twisted. Love must hurt. Then I will know I am alive.

The literary agent and I always had lively dinners at exquisite restaurants he found so there we were seated in an elegant Italian restaurant masquerading as a country bistro.

"It's wonderful how your mother's boyfriend," he said, "took care of her."

"Yes," I said. "Theirs was a real love affair."

"Are you jet lagged?"

"No," I said but I noticed I was having trouble paying attention to the conversation. I was in another world. I kept looking at an older woman who had the same short red hair that my mother had. I was looking at another table where the woman was pretty and flirtatious and I remembered my mother had been like that.

It was becoming clear to me that I had leagues of untold feelings about her. How was I like her? What was the real legacy she left me? Was I as independent, as unable to love?

"I should go," I said. "I'm not quite here."

"I understand," he said.

My friend dropped me off in a cab and as I crossed the street to my apartment building in the cold I could see Arieh standing outside my apartment, like a sentry, with the snow falling around him in the dark.

"What are you doing here?" I asked, as I came up to him. "How long have you been standing outside? It's cold."

"A few hours," he said. Which sounded improbable but then you never knew with him. He complained all the time about his health, but he took long walks in the cold. He never slept. Or, conversely, he took off entire days to sleep. You never knew. He was wearing a camel coat and a fedora hat. He looked like a European grandfather.

"What are you doing?" I asked.

"I'm making a Shiva call."

"The only one," I said, smiling.

We went to a nearby cafe. I stroked his arm. "Oh Arieh," I said, feeling such tenderness. I don't know what kind of tenderness, but tenderness. He had come here and knew that her death was important. Only he and I knew, it seemed, what she had come from, what she had suffered. She herself had refused to know.

I held his arm.

I told him I was going to England to the funeral, where I would know no one except her lover. Arieh was going to Paris, the day I was getting back from England, to see one of his girlfriends.

I told him that the last thing I had said to my mother as she lay in a coma, dying, when I was in London the week before, was, "Such a pretty girl."

He said nothing for a second, remembering the times he'd used that phrase to me.

"Such a pretty girl," as he'd turn my face toward him, sometimes when I was sitting next to him. "Such a pretty girl," when he would be lying down in his shorts and I was sitting fully dressed on his bed, talking about a book I was reading.

I told him that I was reading Jewish prayers at the funeral, even though it was a Christian funeral, even though my mother was being cremated.

"Very Jewish," he said, sarcastically.

"Well, she never cared about that."

He nodded. His parents, too, had disavowed their Judaism, once the war had proved that God never gave up on brutal plans for his chosen people.

But she was Jewish. And I wanted to bring back who she might have been, not who she was.

To my mind, it was my mother's Jewishness that had made her complicated, tortured, brilliant, and too hurt to love her children.

I hung it all on that. At that point, I had nothing else to hang it on.

As I told him these things, I missed the way he would sometimes undo me by cupping my face when we were talking. How he would run his finger along my breast.

I looked up at him.

"Well, I should go to bed," I said.

I said good night and went upstairs alone.

In those days, that didn't strike me as odd.

TEN

"Did you know your mother's lover wrote the TV series, *The Adventures of Robin Hood?*" Arieh asked. It was a Saturday and, as usual, we were sitting outside at a neighborhood restaurant.

The traffic roared by but neither of us noticed it. We were always completely absorbed in each other.

"I can't get over how wonderful Alan was to her," I said. "He took care of her impeccably."

The waiter brought Arieh his usual pork, boudin, cheeses and two loaves of bread.

I looked askance at him, but part of me was amused. Churchill said what an artist needs is audacity. I thought what anyone needs is audacity. And Arieh had it. "Alan also wrote *Two-Way Stretch* and *You Must Be Joking*. I love those movies," Arieh said.

That was the kind of thing Arieh knew.

"I know," I replied. "He's very talented. Witty. But the way he loved her for so long. And took care of her. And now he is alone. I think I should suggest that he and I go to Vienna on a trip so he won't be lonely, as a way of thanking him. I can learn about her there, too."

I liked this idea of my going to Vienna, as if I was rich. I had never been able to take a trip to Europe before on my own funds. My mother had left me a little money, or maybe her Alzheimer's didn't give her time to not leave me the money, and being left even a little money was, to me, like being left the Queen Mary. I could give myself something that I had never been able to give myself.

I would go, like an adult, to Vienna.

"Vienna's still anti-Semitic. When I was there, they wouldn't serve me coffee," he said.

I wasn't sure that was anti-Semitism. It could have been Viennese repulsion at his aggressive manners. He was the antithesis of *gemutlich*.

"But go," he said. "Why not?"

"Yes," I said.

"You look just like your mother in those photos, you know that?" he said. When I had returned from helping Alan clear out her belongings, I had brought back photos of my mother as a young woman. I was proud of her beauty. It was as if it was an heirloom. "I've seen hundreds of pretty Jewish girls like this," he said, when I showed the photos to Arieh.

I had never looked at her in that way.

Then I understood what he was saying. He was telling me I am familiar to him, have a place in history. He can't give me a home with him, but he can give me one with his people.

But, why not with him? I wondered.

He had never married. He had run away from every woman he had ever had an affair with. Always found fault with them, always ended up hating them. That's what intimacy did for him.

"I see," I said.

I called Alan about my Vienna trip idea and he immediately agreed. It made me a bit nervous that Alan kept calling me Daisy, my mother's name, but I figured that's natural in his aroused state of grief. I didn't think that perhaps I liked that he confused us. That maybe this was a way she and I could finally meet.

Alan and I agreed at which small hotel to stay, near the Ringstrasse. When I left three weeks later, I gave Arieh the number.

To my shock, Alan had fallen apart, in the few months since my mother had died. He no longer could walk, his Parkinson's now made it almost impossible for him to move his feet. How did he even get here? I wondered. The will to live, I realized, the power of the will.

Still, I could not imagine how we would travel about together. It was heartbreaking that this tall, brilliant, elegantly dressed, Rex-Harrison-look-alike had so deteriorated.

However, we managed to laboriously sightsee the Belvedere together and then we searched, in a cab, for where my mother had grown up. We found the building that was now in an Arab section, but had once been the Josefstadt section. My mother's building probably had been elegant once, but what struck me was how non-descript it now was. An old building, one you would pass by without notice. This was the home of the mother who had loomed like Snow White's stepmother in my imagination.

Mostly, though, Alan and I had long meals together in tiny restaurants next to the hotel and talked. He would tell me about my mother and about his own life.

He repeated himself often, as old men with impressive pasts often do.

After these meals, we would go to our respective rooms to sleep.

That's when Arieh would call, with a map of Vienna up on his computer screen. Each night, I told him where I went when my mother's boyfriend took his afternoon nap. To the modern Museum and all the Schiele paintings. To a *Missa Solemnis* concert in a church. To the Jewish museum where I learned that fewer Austrian Jews returned after the war than Jews from any other occupied country.

"Don't become Jewish," Alan said to me. "Don't get interested in it."

Was this the infamous anti-Semitism that Arieh spent his time railing about? But then my mother had been Jewish so how could Alan be anti-Semitic? "Well, she was, "I could hear

Arieh say emphatically, "a self-hating Jew. It was common then. But people like that can't be happy."

Was he right? I was neither a self-hating nor self-committed Jew and I wasn't that happy so what did all this mean?

"Why not a Jew?" I asked Alan.

"You don't want to do that," Alan replied in his clipped English accent.

I could hear Arieh in my mind. "See? See?" he would say. "They all are. They all are."

I didn't like that Alan was dismissing a people like that. Why shouldn't I want to become Jewish?

On top of that, I was missing Arieh. Someone I could talk to. Someone, who in his own loneliness, had made himself part of my story. The only pleasure of the trip was his nightly phone call. Because he listened to me.

I told Arieh how Alan kept asking if I remembered that weekend in Rome or in Quebec City. He would look shocked when I would say, "No, Alan, it's me, Mira, not Daisy."

"Oh yes," he'd say. Then he'd look very suspiciously at me as if he didn't believe me.

Then I told Arieh that Alan had said, when I asked him what my mother's political beliefs were, "Ignorance."

"Like you," Arieh said, on the phone.

I told Arieh how one night, at dinner, my mother's eighty-year-old boyfriend said, "Why don't we sleep together?"

I didn't think Alan was capable of having sex but, as I mentioned before, the will.

My best friend and other friends had told me before I left New York that Alan would do that. Want to sleep with me. I refused to believe them. He loved my mother. I was her daughter. He wouldn't do such a thing. I refused to listen to anyone because this time, I thought, it will be different.

He will talk to me and advise me on how to make my life work. I will learn about her and thus maybe learn about why I am the way I am.

In other words, I wanted my mother's boyfriend to be parental in the way she never had been.

That's why I didn't listen to anyone.

But instead, as my father used to say, "Like goes to like." My mother hadn't wanted to be a mother. And my *comme il faut* stepfather didn't want his role either.

"We can't," I said to Alan, gently. "You're my mother's boyfriend. She might look down from heaven and smite me."

"But she left you to me," he said. "It was a codicil in her will."

When I told Arieh about Alan's request on the phone that night, he, uncharacteristically, made no comment.

But he called back much later, a little drunk, and said; "I just had dinner with Bob Peters. His wife is in China and mine is in Vienna."

I smiled.

"How can I be your wife? We don't sleep together and we always fight."

"Sounds like a perfect marriage," he said.

A few hours after I returned from the trip, Arieh came down that night to see me. He knew we had achieved an unusual intimacy on those calls. With an ocean between us, we had not sparred. As soon as I went to meet him out on the street, I rubbed my hand on his stomach, as I always did, as if it were a genie's lamp.

He said, unusually, "Come sleep with me."

Our intimacy on the phone had given him the courage.

"No," I said, "I'm tired."

He looked hurt. "You never can do anything normal can you?" he said.

"I'm tired," I said feebly.

"Of course you are," he said sarcastically and, even though we went out and had dinner, he was aloof and withholding in conversation.

That weekend, I went to his apartment on the way to one of our lunches and we were on his bed, chatting. I was waiting for him to put on a clean shirt so we could go out. But instead he sat down next to me on the bed and began to undo my blouse and caress my breasts. "You don't know how beautiful you are, do you?" he said.

"Why do you always say that?" I asked.

He began kissing my breasts which let's face it is a wonderful feeling. My mind said, Why not? And then I noticed he had an erection and when I put my hand on him, I was surprised at what a lovely size it was, big but not too big, and he said, "Why don't we make love?"

Our arms were all over each other and we were nuzzling, happily.

I nodded.

So we both got naked and he was inside me and he was gentle with kisses and yet aggressive, which I liked, and in its way it was tender and loving and everything was surprisingly normal, since I always had this fear he did not like women or even me, and, when we were finished, it was then I began to feel maybe we could be a couple. Maybe he is not twisted.

I ignored the cross dressing past, the anger, the quixoticness. Maybe it would all work out.

At lunch after making love, I was quiet, smiling at him and listening to his every word with joyous presence. He said, "Look at you. You're in love."

"I know," I said. "I've become so stupid. I can't say anything. This is terrible."

"Yes," he laughed. "This is it. You will never be the same again. You will just be stupid and love me."

I smiled, daftly. I was mesmerized. By what? I suddenly had hope; hope that I could have all that intimacy and sexuality in one man. Maybe I could have a man who understands me and knows me and we could even have a loving sex life. Maybe he could be a man for me.

We walked holding hands along First Avenue through a street fair. It was raining. "I love the rain," he said. And I told him how the poet Fernando Pessoa had one of his characters love the rain, for the falling down of sadness on him.

"Is he Brazilian?" he asked.

"No. Portuguese."

"Almost the same," he said.

At dinner, I stared at Arieh rapturously. I spent the night with him and I fell asleep on his chest, his chest that I so loved.

He was gentle with me.

Two days later, he suggested we go to Israel. He wanted to introduce me to the country, the places, and the people that meant the most to him. He began looking into trips but nothing was decided.

I got a job interview and the second interview was scheduled two weeks ahead.

"I have to meet with them on the 26th."

"But that's when we're going to Israel."

"But we don't have a firm date," I said. "You never gave me any dates."

He hung up on me.

This time, it hurt. This time, I was invested in him.

After a week of silence, I called him and said, "Why, why are you not speaking to me?"

"You're crazy and cruel," he said, "and I cannot be bothered anymore."

And he hung up again.

I called back and he said, "I am not interested in you."

Maybe, in his odd way, he had been reaching out when he said, Let's go to Israel. Maybe I hadn't heard him properly.

True, he was not clear about the dates or whether we were going, but worse, I was the same. I had not been specific either.

That must have hurt him, I told myself.

What was wrong with me?

We were now, it seemed, singing the same tune and the song was called: *How Could She Do It?*

ELEVEN

That was how it began.

And now two years later . . . Michael, the nice Englishman, tells me about decisions he is making in refinancing one of his projects. He speaks very softly and I cannot follow the story. There is no humor or irony to it, as with his other stories.

"You are not interested in me," Michael finally said, as I looked glumly at him over my meal.

I moved my eyes toward the back of the restaurant, to the banquette mirror. Why am I so sad?

"I don't know," I said.

After dinner, standing out on Park Avenue, Michael put me in a cab and stuffed $10 down my shirt for the cab. He slammed the taxi door shut. God, he must have thought, she is so bloody frustrating. She won't get involved. She hasn't a clue how to be in a relationship.

When I got home and out onto my busy street, I clicked open my phone to call Arieh. It was a compulsion.

At first, he sounded happy to hear from me but then he started. "You fucked him. You loved me but you fucked him."

"That was over a year ago."

"It will never be over," he said. "My life is over. You ruined my life. I should have died 23 years ago."

"Why 23?"

"That's when I lost Barbara. I should have married her and had children with her. Now I have nothing and then I had to meet you. You who destroyed me."

Then I began, walking round the block, thinking I would talk him down from his demonic possession. I didn't realize I was walking the block to help myself. "Listen," I said, "that is the past. There are 28 years left for us, you say, so why not go for now, for love, make something and live instead of hiding in the past. I love you and we can build something."

"No I will always live with you and your boyfriend. You disgusting pieces of shit."

"No, now. Stay in now. Now we can make something."

"I don't want to," he said. "Not with someone as insane as you. Why would I want that?"

And he hung up.

About 4.45 in the morning my phone started ringing in the dark. I knew who it was. No one rational would call me at that hour. I picked it up.

"Listen," Arieh said. "Because of you I had nightmares last night. Stay away from me. I will never stop abusing you. I will never ever forgive you. What you did is unforgivable."

He called me five times to tell me more or less the same. I am inhuman, a monster, evil, to be stayed away from. "What do you think about that?" he asked.

"I'm sorry," I said.

"I will never forgive you," he replied.

Then silence.

Or maybe not.

TWELVE: My Crime

We'd have to go back to that summer day when Arieh asked me to drive him to deliver files to his client, Michael Patterson.

Michael was alone at his sprawling, sunlit house in Connecticut, and came down from his garden to meet us as we drove up. He shook hands with me and I commented on the prettiness of his house, with its blue exterior, sitting on a hill.

He had lunch set out for us at a table on one of his porches; wine, ham, cheese, French bread. We sat down and I felt a bit shy but Arieh was always wonderful for that, talking away volubly, about what films he'd seen, how terrible the court system was in New York City, judges whom he admired, judges who were idiots.

Michael laughed at Arieh's storytelling.

Arieh said to me at lunch, "I had to prepare Michael once for court and get him to explain in plain English his three degrees from Cambridge. Can you imagine? I thought it would intimidate the judge."

"Yes," Michael said, smiling.

Being British, Michael turned to me politely, and began asking gently insinuating questions. Arieh tells me you play the piano. What do you play? Do you really? You come from Canada? Questions like that.

I answered quietly and uncomfortably. I don't like talking about myself in chit chat sentences. It never sounds real. Arieh was the one for endless stories. Arieh would inflate whatever I said. "Yes, she has seen as many movies as I have." Which I hadn't. "Yes, she reads all the time. Novels." And so on.

I studied Michael as they talked about law cases they had worked on together. Michael was shorter, I saw, than Arieh, slender, with long fair hair. He wore round glasses and looked like an aged Harry Potter. The sunlight bounced off his conservative expensive blue shirt and bleached it almost white in the sun.

As I handed Michael the mustard, he said, "Since you read so much, tell me, why hasn't anyone written about what women feel about men?"

"Plenty have. Especially French writers," I said, shocked he didn't know that.

Even so, I liked the question.

On the drive home, Arieh teased me about having fallen in love with Michael.

"Yes, it's true," I said. I had thought, Michael is my kind of man.

I had thought about it academically. It is easy to think of possibilities with someone not available. Arieh told me Michael was married.

Arieh and I were, as usual, constantly having lunches and dinners together. He began inviting Michael to join us. I would be a little embarrassed, because I did find Michael attractive, for his subtlety, for his discretion. I had the feeling there was plenty of sex around him. I didn't know why but somehow I felt he had mistresses, maybe even went to prostitutes. All that repression and all that studying at Winchester and Cambridge must create intense sexual furor, I imagined.

Arieh said, as we walked away from one of these lunches, "You would never know with him. He's too English."

I agreed, but felt I knew.

Sometimes alone at dinner with Arieh, I would say, "I only see you so I can see Michael."

Arieh laughed and said, "I know."

Perhaps Arieh was, unconsciously, setting me up to throw me away. You never knew about that either.

Michael and I both played the piano. He was better than me by about forty years. His piano was made for him in Luxembourg. He told us the story, as we sat on his porch that first day, how he had gone into all these piano shops in Luxembourg. Then he found the one he wanted built for him. It broke apart as it was being shipped and he told the story of its reconstruction in his country house living room with loving detail.

I sat next to him on the piano bench as he played some Liszt whom he loved. He encouraged me to play for us but I wouldn't. I am not that good.

He recommended his piano teacher to me, and since I instinctively trusted him, I began taking lessons with his teacher.

Maria turned out to be a good piano teacher but she had one idiosyncrasy. She liked to gossip.

"Mikel," she said in her Russian accent, "too fast play. He take very difficult piece and ruin it."

I hated to think what she told him about my own virtuosity.

Then she sighed. "I was in love with Mikel when was dying my husband," she said, lamenting. "He was coming here and we would be speaking. I feed him chocolate. Why is he not with wife?"

"I don't know." I was also curious but I've told myself that one cannot judge a marriage. People have all kinds of twisted agreements to keep them interested.

Maria is 76, a short round Babushka woman whom you would pass on the street and never notice. You'd think, another old woman walking by.

"I cannot live without sex," she said, pounding her fist on the piano.

This was to explain the demented Czech ex-fighter who lived with her. He was strong looking, a bull, as they say, and was always messing about in the kitchen.

"He knows nothing of the piano," she said. She pointed to her head and said, "He is very stupid."

But she also added, "He is unbelievable."

"How?"

"He wants to have sex constantly."

And then I saw, I saw that her dark eyes gleamed, her smile was mischievous. I saw that her soul was wild with love.

That afternoon at Michael's country house with its many porches surrounded by enormous trees, Michael and Arieh swam in the pool and Michael told me to go get the Madeira out of the kitchen cabinet. I bowed to him before going over to get it and he kept giving me orders in that upper class British voice.

He laughed at my feigned submission.

I did not know then that his wife never listened to a word he said.

Arieh had told me Michael's wife spends her summers in her own house in Canada. They are never together. It was, in Arieh's mind, a bizarre marriage. If I were married to Arieh, I'd spend most of my life in Beirut just for some peace and quiet so I didn't think it so bizarre.

I set the three glasses on the side of the pool and Michael swam energetically and Arieh, who is a big man, as you know, swam with his tiny goggles on which made him look like some enormous sting ray and he kept looking up at me to see what I was doing.

A year later, Michael self-published his book about symbolism during the Renaissance and I offered to help him promote it, even though I knew it was a lost cause.

So we sat, the three of us, after a few drinks, at one of Arieh's and my restaurants, and came up with ideas. I made an illegible list on the paper tablecloth. Occult societies. Links with Renaissance sites, and so on. I ripped the list off for him.

Yet I did not have much hope for Michael's book. The fact was that Michael's book had pictures from the Renaissance books he collected, but no original research, thus it was a mishmash of already published information, and so of no real interest to anyone. We devised a campaign to email humanities professors about it.

At dinner, Michael decided against a book party. It occurred to me, fleetingly, like a wisp across the mind, that this plotting about his book was just a way for us all to get together.

I thought maybe he was attracted to me. After all, his wife is gone and I am paying attention to his book.

I am not the only one who suffers from vanity.

However, Michael was never untoward toward me since he thought I was seeing Arieh.

He did not know that Arieh could be very cruel or that he'd been a cross dresser. He also didn't know we had gone back to not sleeping together. Mostly we argued, which Arieh once again said showed we were destined for marriage. It's just that I'd had that marriage already.

But, as the publicity idea meetings went on, Arieh stopped talking to me. The first reason was that I was talking on my cellphone when he said he was going to call me right back. Then it was that I vote Democratic. "You and your friends," he said, "in your liberal ideas are responsible for the Khmer Rouge, the Vietnam Boat People, the Taliban and other world atrocities."

That's where Arieh went when he wanted to distance himself from the world. To political atrocities. We were all to blame.

Our so-called romance was about finished when Michael told Arieh he wanted to continue plotting ideas for marketing his book.

Arieh said, "Call her directly."

Our first dinner alone, Michael brought a list of things for us to talk about.

I was a bit flustered and had worn my favorite black dress, which has many crossing straps above my chest that makes me feel like Coco Chanel.

The restaurant was elegant and, as we walked in, his hand touched the skin of my back. It felt like a date. I was frightened. Maybe we would have nothing to say without Arieh. Two introverts, like Michael and myself, can rest while Arieh declaims the whole world.

Michael and I began by going down his list about his book and then I, being curious about him, took to asking him personal questions.

"Were you married before?" I asked.

"Yes," he said. "My first wife is quite a well known sculptor. She was young when she married me; she's my cousin, actually. She left me for another man. The man she ran off with was on his honeymoon when he met her."

"Ah . . ." I was busy taking in his double-breasted navy blue jacket. This elegance made me happy. It reminded me of long ago European relatives. Or maybe that he paid attention to beauty, even his own. Maybe he was not self-destructive.

"What about you?" he asked. "What about your divorce?"

"It was difficult. It took me a long time to get over."

He said surprisingly, "I wish I could get divorced."

I said, "No you don't."

He said, "I do. She is very mean."

At which point, I thought maybe he was mean. People usually ascribe to other people their own traits. And Michael was alone all the time at the many dinners I had with him and Arieh. Where was his wife? In my mind he was cruel in abandoning her like that.

The waiter placed our Dover soles in front of us. This was English, the kind of meal I would have had with my father. I had a twang of missing my father, deeply. My pal. The man who raised me. British and wild, the man who had been my home.

"Rabelais," I said (knowing he was Michael's favorite author), "says that you have a perfect marriage."

"What do you mean?"

"Freedom but someone always there."

He nodded.

I didn't say that Rabelais also thought men should marry much younger women to stay young. I was only ten years younger than Michael.

I did say, "He also thought that women had to be replastered, boiled in a cauldron or something, to regain their youthful beauty. Obviously he foresaw plastic surgery."

Michael didn't respond.

He said, "You and Arieh should come again to the country."

I said, "He is not speaking to me."

"You could come anyway. Even not speaking."

I smiled.

"What are you reading?" I asked.

He said he was reading a book on the origin of symbols and he said that no one knows why snakes have been used as a symbol throughout history. Why snakes in every myth and religion?

I said nothing but that night I had an erotic dream where I kissed him and he had a forked tongue.

We met for a drink the next week to discuss his book even more. I was on my way to the symphony and we picked a bar close to Lincoln Center, with a big picture of a sensual woman hanging over us. We sat up at the bar and he knocked back some Campari and sodas, and after a few minutes, he said, "When are we doing this again?"

I stared straight ahead and pretended I didn't notice this flirting. He was married. He was Arieh's friend.

"Well I have a lot of freelance writing most nights."

"I'll have to give you an assignment to see you," he said.

As his errant publicist, I set up a dinner with Nancy who was an agent friend of mine, Michael and myself, in hopes that Nancy would help Michael with his book. I even invited Arieh because he and Michael were friends.

Arieh agreed to go for Michael's sake.

Nancy was a friend not only of mine, but she had also met Arieh through her own network of friends. She and I often went out together for drinks and to chat about how impossible it was to meet a man who was interesting and how maybe we didn't want to be tied down anyway. But she liked expensive free dinners. I thought, Why not? Maybe all of us will get something out of this. If nothing else, sexual energy. Michael's possible attraction to me. My forbidden possible attraction to Michael. My war of attraction to Arieh. Nancy's possible attraction to either of them. Arieh's attraction to anger, complimentarily provided by me.

We'd all get something out of it.

When I met Michael and Arieh at the restaurant, I kissed Michael on the cheek and shook hands with Arieh. Arieh, after all, was as usual not speaking to me.

Arieh began, as we four sat down at our table, telling us the number of people fascists have killed over the centuries and I said, "It sounds like an excellent way of population control."

I was surprised and confused when Michael put his hand on my knee during dinner.

It turned out to be a dull dinner; Nancy had no interest in a book on symbolism during the Renaissance. I tried to tell Michael she wouldn't, no agent would. I said to Michael, "If it was a book about how many people you have slept with who are interested in the Renaissance, you'd have a better chance."

Michael invited us all up to the country. Arieh and Nancy bowed out.

I didn't go either. It didn't seem appropriate to go up alone. Instead, I stayed home and sat on my fire escape and read and spent an undue amount of time thinking about Michael. I was smitten with his constant, slightly witty emails. I cried when I got to the part in the novel I was reading where the lovers come together.

I berated myself for being old and not beautiful anymore. For not being able to undo a man.

As if he heard me, on Monday he called and said politely, but forcefully, "Why don't you come and visit next weekend?"

And I said, very civilized, but somewhat breathlessly, "Yes I'll come up on Sunday."

At this age, I told myself, I should just dive in. Anywhere.

He said his nephew and nephew's girlfriend would also be there.

It crossed my mind that there was a time when men conspired to be alone with me.

I decided that Michael's intentions were honorable, unlike mine. And mine maybe weren't quite so dishonorable because I asked Arieh if he would like to come.

"No," he said. "You go."

I took the train to the country and Michael was waiting at the station. As he took my bag, he said, "You look very lovely. Your hair matches your skirt."

"It does?"

I was surprised at a compliment.

In the car, I pulled the hem of my skirt up towards my hair to check if the colors were alike. To me they did not match but I am fastidious. A *yekketah*.

His wife was blonde. I am dark haired. To him, the colors matched.

When we arrived at his house, he showed me my room in a corner of his house. The room was formerly his daughter's, with a framed picture of Tom Cruise on her desk. For a moment I mistakenly thought that the photo was Michael in his youth. My bedroom was far from his room.

My mind was weaving constantly as I looked at the garden; as I listened to him play Tchaikovsky on the piano. His long fingers are delicate and he played with intent focus. He played extremely well, and feelingly, although too fast, as Maria said. His playing fast was a sign of willfulness, I later realized, his insisting the music be played at his own tempo, not the composer's. But who am I to make any comment on willfulness?

After he had played and I unpacked, we sat by the pool, we four, Michael, his nephew and nephew's girlfriend and drank tequila and talked of films, the fate of short stories, and we spoke of books. I learned that young people are not thinking of books. They are thinking of films and the net.

Michael said, "Who is reading all the philosophy books in Barnes and Noble?"

He writes them himself and did not try to get them published.

I didn't know what to tell him.

"Students. Obsessed people."

I thought but didn't say, "People don't even read novels of love anymore."

After this little discussion, I decided to drink in the last vestiges of sun on one of his porches. Michael stayed downstairs with his nephew and nephew's girlfriend. They were looking at a map of the area.

The porch that still had sun on it was off his bedroom. I decided to read there anyway. I was wearing a bikini which perhaps I should not wear anymore but who cared? Who cared?

When his nephew and nephew's girlfriend went for a walk, Michael came up to the porch.

I stood up and sat next to him on the railing. He pulled me toward him to kiss me.

I remembered the dream of the erotic kiss and the forked tongue. I had asked him about it in an email.

"It's obvious," he had responded.

I brought it up on the porch again. "You know my dream didn't necessarily mean something sexual," I said a bit unconvinced myself.

"Oh come on," he said.

"It could be me embracing a part of myself since Jung believes every character in a dream is yourself," but it probably took about twenty seconds before I was exploring his forked tongue in reality.

About an hour later, when his relatives returned, we came downstairs together and my hair was askew and Michael and I were slightly embarrassed together.

I have done something stupid, I realized.

Arieh doesn't want me anyway, I told myself. Arieh has told me that in no uncertain terms. Just the other night, he had yelled at me that I was a piece of shit after a dinner where we argued about Hemingway's writing. I had told Arieh I could not stand these discussions about films, books, these lectures of his. Then he walked off.

He was always walking off.

I don't know why I had told Arieh I hated those discussions since those are the very subjects I like to discuss. But I hated being lectured. Arieh had said, "You're just looking to start a fight."

Isn't it Arieh who starts fights?

This man, I said to myself as I looked to Michael that afternoon in the country, seems to like me. He's intelligent and he's erudite. Why not, for a change, someone who likes me?

THIRTEEN

Two weeks later, I went again to Michael's. This time there were no relatives. He picked me up at the train in the early evening and we were more relaxed. He made dinner as soon as we got to the house and I am someone who usually does not like to eat at home, but I was willing to withstand this intimacy, and he cooked lamb and sprouts, a British dinner. At the sink, we would fall into each other's arms and kiss. At the counter. Every time we passed each other, getting a tomato, or a serving spoon, we had our hands on each other. I hadn't been this responsive to a man since the first year with my husband.

"Your skirt is so sexy," he said.

"It is?"

"The material." It was a sort of nylon material, soft.

This is a man of sensuality.

"You're amazingly sensual," he said.

We are always seeing ourselves.

I had a scotch to relax me. Maybe it would keep me to myself.

"If you are such a Platonist," I said at our candlelight dinner in the kitchen, "why aren't we having a platonic relationship?"

"Exactly. I am discussing this in my dialogues on Plato. The answer is that you are to blame."

"You should be like St. Augustine and swear off," I said. God knows it would make my life easier, I thought.

"The dialogues I am writing are about that. She is the one thinking of love in terms of feeling and he is theoretical. Everything, of course, gets into a mix up. I thought the two people would be called Charles and Diana."

"Not Charles and Diana," I said. It seemed too trendy, although I didn't say it.

"I like those Black names," he said, "like Tatiana and Tiffany."

"She should have a very sensual name and he the name of an academic," I said.

"You mean like Aphrodite and Augustin?" he asked.

I thought I better keep quiet. I should know better than to talk to someone about their creative process.

Later we watched the end of *The Battle of Algiers* in his tiny television room that was like a hidden bunker with blankets and pillows. "You could hide me from the Nazis here," I said, stupidly.

The Nazis could find this room. I did. And, given what was going to happen, they did find it. I eventually got tortured and died, in my way, for this lapse of judgment, sleeping with Michael, Arieh's friend.

I had seen the film before so I didn't miss not seeing it and Michael never saw it because we got taken up with other things. The last time I had snuggled and gone onto other matters on a sofa in front of a movie I didn't watch was with my husband over fifteen years ago.

This was another woman's husband. I had to keep this in mind, although it was easy to forget being alone with him in the country.

We slept in separate beds, their beds, next to each other. I had never been with anyone who would even consider owning twin beds. I was shocked but, in a way, liked the pristine privacy of it.

In the morning he climbed in with me. He was like a young man in his energy toward me.

"Did you sleep well?" he asked.

"Not at first, but then. You?"

"No I got up at three and worked. Made notes."

"Was it having a foreigner in your house?"

"Not at all," he said, hugging me.

It seemed to me he was practicing his piano scales on my body. It seemed as if, because he can see nothing without his glasses, he was touching me into words.

Arieh always told me I was fat. He liked to look at me as a disappointment, was quick to point out a flaw. Fat ass, crooked feet, which he would follow up with the usual compliment, "You're the most beautiful woman in the world." But my mind, as he intended, only registered where I was wanting.

Michael kept remarking on how slender I was.

Which one of them was telling the truth? In a way, both of them. I am both. Round and slight. Repressed and passionate. Frightened and heedless. Therein lie all my problems.

Michael made coffee that morning and we looked at his paintings, ones he did between marriages. He said he would give me one for my birthday. There I was looking out at the trees from his kitchen and then at his paintings on his walls and then listening to him on the piano, a Chopin piece that made me cry.

Finally I turned to him and said, "I had no idea being a mistress was this pleasurable. Why did I wait so long?"

He laughed, delighted. "You have all the freedom."

He did not realize, because he is married, that the freedom is not that interesting. It is the tension that is interesting.

We went off to our different work areas and worked. He loved to work. I always wanted a man who loved to work.

To sober myself, I said, before he left for his office at the other end of the house, "What is your wife doing this weekend?"

"Reading Baron's in bed, taking her belly dancing class, and she goes to church on Sunday."

She was at church while I was kissing her husband.

"Do you feel guilty?" I asked.

"Not at all. We haven't spent time together in 10 years. I wouldn't mind leaving her, I told you. She has never lifted a finger to make this marriage work. She has her own house for

God's sake. Never goes on holiday with me. Never comes here. We haven't slept together in 10 years. She is impossible."

I was silent, thinking about all this. Did he drive her away?

"Don't worry about us. Things will work out," he said.

When we took a break, we went downstairs to look at his paintings that were covered up in plastic so I could choose one for my apartment. I didn't really like the paintings. They were stiff. They looked like colored architectural drawings but what I liked was that he painted them. And maybe also I liked that I would not live with the man himself, but with his art. Wasn't that what I always wanted? I always had trouble dealing with a real person.

FOURTEEN

Two weeks later, after a period of silence, Arieh called me. My punishment must be over, I thought. I could not remember what I had done that time to be punished.

But things had changed since I last saw him. I was sleeping with his client.

It's not that I didn't realize that first afternoon alone in the country with Michael that I was ruining it with Arieh. But I thought, Why not? Arieh doesn't want a relationship with me. He has told me that I am nothing to him.

"Hi," Arieh said on the phone.

"How are you?" I asked.

"Well I still have my imaginary illnesses and imaginary pain."

"And what else are you imagining?" I asked.

"I am imagining that I have many classes to get my masters of law and I am imagining that I need more clerical help in my office. Why are you so inarticulate?" he asked.

"I don't want you to attack me."

"I absolutely promise I won't," he said. "I swear on ten lifetimes that I will not."

Did he not mean anything he said?

"Well, ask me a question," I replied.

"Do you believe the Italian lire will be devalued in the European Union?"

"I don't believe the European Union will last."

"Ah. For once we agree," he said delightedly.

Then he asked me a complicated legal question that I inadvertently got right.

"I must go," I said. "I have to work."

"At this hour?" It was night. About 10 pm.

"Yes."

"What are you doing?" he asked.

Then my call waiting beeped.

"Hold on a minute," I said to Arieh.

"Hello?"

"Yeahhhhhh, I found you a bed."

"Joey. I'm on the phone."

"Of course, you're on the phone. Don't, don't tell me you're going to call me right back. I can't stand it."

"What should I do then?"

"Call me when you actually want to look at this bed."

"Okay. Thanks—"

Then I switched back to Arieh.

"What were you saying?" I asked.

"What are you working on?"

"I have work for clients," I said on the phone. "I'm a working girl."

"Be careful to whom you're saying that."

I smiled.

"So what ARE you doing?" he asked again. After all, he is a lawyer.

"Nothing that is interesting at all. Nothing that would interest you or me in the least."

"You have no idea what interests me."

I thought he meant that I interested him.

Then he said, "I saw the worst film yesterday. A French one. It was so slow that the most exciting point was when someone in the audience's cellphone rang."

I snickered a bit.

"You know I need to be with someone," I said. "I need to get married."

"I know."

"Why don't you want to marry me?" I asked, teasing, because I was pretty sure he could never be married. It wasn't in his nature. He could never be that consistent.

"Who said I didn't?"

"Well it could be worse," I said, because I had no idea what to say.

"What?"

"You could be married."

He sighed.

"You could do a lot worse than me," I said. Maybe I was trying to lay the groundwork about my seeing Michael.

"I know," he said.

And then he abruptly hung up with that swirl of drama where the magician disappears into his cape.

FIFTEEN

A month later, Michael and I were sitting side by side in a restaurant banquette at lunch. I was working next door in a company that I couldn't stand and I felt the pressure of having to get back to the ridiculous furor of managers racing around believing that the entire world could not wait one extra minute for every panic-stricken idea they came up with. This fervorous self-hype was because no one was waiting at all.

I looked over at Michael, settling into his banquette with a quiet smile, and noticed he had that languorousness of someone who does not punch a clock, who does not have to worry about money.

We ordered and then Michael said very firmly, but out of the blue, "I am leaving my wife. I have told her."

"You have?" I swallowed, surprised. Then I became terrified. Events were unfolding rather too quickly, weren't they?

Drily, he said, "I am a man of action. Here I've met a woman who is beautiful and sexy and fun to be with so what else can I do?"

In the first place, it was not a pleasant way to hear myself described. Did he not see the impossibilities, the difficulties within me? The fears that precluded a lifetime of mistakes? Did he not have any idea who I was? It seemed he was giving a magazine description of me, a stupid magazine. And these traits he was listing didn't seem reasons to leave anyone's wife.

"What is there to decide?" he asked, smiling, victoriously. He had made a decision. A new life was before him.

"What do you mean?" I asked quietly.

His reply came in a mild voice, but oddly clipped. "My marriage is a disaster. My wife is crazy. She doesn't do anything I want. My daughter's grown. Of course, I should leave."

Aha. What I heard was, That's that. Done. Onto the next.

The waiter placed my shrimp salad before me.

Michael said, "Thank you" to him, with that hyphenated British accent that makes one think everything in the world is in order.

"Well," I said, "I'm a bit crazy too. I mean I haven't been good at relationships. I'm not good at committing . . ."

"Nonsense," he countered. "You just haven't been with the right person before."

It's true. He was remarkably different from my previous lovers, including my husband. Michael was the first man I had been with who had enough self-esteem to become successful. He had that graspingness, that groundedness to make money. He played the piano. He was accomplished. He was educated.

Could it be true? That I was alone because I had heretofore met a rush of baboons?

"But we've got to figure out how to be together," Michael continued intently, while picking at his sole. "We should live together, find a place. Which is very difficult.

"To find somewhere we both like."

I nodded.

"We could have a special room for you where you could do whatever you like. One for me. We could have a fireplace, somewhere really lovely."

I tried to smile. He was rushing me, rushing me to practicalities, even if they were sugar coated.

He wants me to fill in for his wife.

"That's not the problem," I said. "It's the emotional part that is hard. Do you want to change your life now? Leave all that is familiar? The guilt. That part is hard."

I was remembering how my own divorce had wracked me.

"No, the emotions take care of themselves," he said, much to my surprise. "It's taking care of the physical changes that are difficult. Where to go. Furnishing the place. All of that."

I laughed, unbelieving. You're focusing on furniture when leaving your wife of thirty years?

What about HER feelings?

What if I don't work out, I thought.

"We must move forward," he said.

I sipped my water. My god, where are we going?

Weeks before, when we had been driving back from his country house and I was kissing him in the car and holding his hand and generally purring about everything, even in the middle of a traffic jam, purring because I love motion, I said, "God we're acting like we're in love."

And he said, "Aren't we?"

But I meant in love with life. Not one person. I've never been able to love one person only. Life has always called in larger landscapes to me.

I told myself that it would take a while for him to put this plan into action and new events would unfold. I would do, as I had always done, nothing.

Arieh and I met one day shortly after this to have a drink. I had just left work and we were by the Helmsley Hotel. He was going to a party afterwards. There was something about being with him that made me feel happy. Maybe his sadness allowed me to acknowledge my own sadness. Maybe his not belonging anywhere made me feel less alone about how I didn't belong anywhere either.

The truth is I have never met anyone so similar to me. We are both emotional, impatient, spontaneous, lone wolves. Or maybe a better way to put it is we are both children. I just wasn't as depressed. Or was I?

Once he said to me, "You're difficult, but I'm impossible."

Arieh and I walked along the street and he was complaining. "I am cursed," he said. "I have nothing. No money. No home.

I should have kept the apartment I owned twenty years ago but no, I sold it. Because I was sick. I should have died 24 years ago."

I had heard this so many times, I didn't get alarmed. He always exaggerated when he spoke. According to him, he was in constant emotional and physical pain. I thought he was fishing for affirmation, a reincarnation of Sarah Bernhardt's over-dramatizing.

I also thought he was talking about me. I thought he was telling me he needed my love.

It shows how self-centered I was.

I ventured a response to his complaining, "I don't sleep with you because I am seeing someone else."

I told him this to explain that by rights I should be loving him, given how embroiled we were. I should have been making him dinner. Being kind to him. Holding him in bed while he studied for his tax degree. I wanted him to know I didn't do all these things not because I didn't love him, but because I was seeing someone else.

I was aware the logic was frail, but it was true.

"Why should I care?" he responded.

And a few minutes later, he told me he had to leave early for this party he was going to.

An hour later, Arieh called me on the cellphone. I was ambling round Saks before I was to meet Michael. Trying to find that rare brand of makeup that would take twenty years off my face.

Arieh was crying on the phone. My heart stopped at the sound of his tears. So did the whirl of people in Saks. "What is it?" I said.

"I can't live without you," he said.

"But you're always telling me you don't like me," I replied.

"You're such a child," and he hung up.

"Why is he like this?" Michael asked me, sitting on my couch later that night, and I was telling him guiltily about Arieh's emotional outburst.

"I must take care of him," I said. "I must be kind to him." My hand was on Michael's grey flannel trousers, stroking his delicate upper leg, as I tried to explain my relation to Arieh in terms, which made no sense. My skirt seemed to be riding up my thighs of its own volition.

"I've known him all these years," Michael said, "and he was perfectly normal in business. I noticed he never married but I thought that was just luck. Meeting the right person."

I dismissed the thought that Michael was turning out to be one of those people who does not look deeply into personality.

I began my explanation.

"When I was a child," I said, "my father told me my Austrian mother was Jewish and I would have been gassed by Hitler. I proceeded to go on a rampage of dreams. My father was tied to a chair and the Nazis, as my punishment, would force me to watch him being hit and burned and beaten to death. That was the worst torture they could inflict. But Arieh's mother really has been in Auschwitz, it was no dream, she has a number on her arm, and I am sure he has witnessed her actual torture every day in his mind since the day he became conscious. It has fractured him."

Michael looked at me quizzically.

"Is this why you like dreams so much?" he asked.

"No. I like the symbolism."

"Which is why you related to my book," he said.

"Yes."

"Why do you like symbols?"

"The imagination is so various. Images are stronger than reality."

I thought that maybe he was beginning to see he had on his hands a woman whose mind was not moving like other people's. I imagined he liked it sexually, he liked the seeming freedom of it, the possibility of desire for him, in my obvious discombobulation, but could he live with all that internal clamoring? He who had been hidden behind his desk.

Michael continued, "I was not unhappy practicing the piano by myself and researching and writing all alone in the country till I met you. Now I am not happy."

"You will live longer," I said, trying to change the subject, "if you are happy," knowing this would have some affect on him. He was careful with his health.

"Yes," he said, "studies prove that."

Suddenly I realized that, while I had not been paying attention, it had become my duty to make him happy. He wanted a life with a woman who would spend her time with him and was loving and responsible to him. He wanted this. He, sweetly, was even willing to do his best to make me happy in response for this world of consistent warmth in which I was to immerse him.

I noticed I didn't feel too happy about it.

I kissed him goodbye when he left, happy he was leaving.

How can I make any of us happy, I thought. I don't even know what it is.

SIXTEEN

"Hello Daisy?" I heard in a soft English tremor asked as I picked up the phone.

"No, Alan, it's Mira." I pushed the phone closer up to my ear so I could hear him. He was so faint all the way from England and this many years from his time of virility.

"Right," he said. "Well I love you darling."

He sounded so forlorn so I said, "I love you too."

What harm could it do? I was half way 'round the world.

And that was how it happened that Alan, my dead mother's boyfriend, who couldn't walk even one city block, and certainly not up my stairs, ended up arriving in New York on a whim, like a rushing lover, and taking a taxi from the airport to my building, not really knowing why he was here, and I ended up having to find him a hotel.

Which I did. An inexpensive one because I didn't want New York to clip him like it does everyone else. I didn't want this last act of romantic valor on his part making a fool of him. So I stuck him in a Ramada hotel in the Korean neighborhood. That was the best value.

Thus he was on my hands for the next seven days. I had to spend the daytime at that dreaded job, and in the evening I went to his hotel where he shuffled himself to the edge of his Ramada Inn bed, trying to get me to talk about my feelings which I couldn't because some part of me did not want intimacy with, of all people, him, my mother's lover. I mean, could he be trusted? What had he really seen about her?

But since he was a type of relative to me, I began ferrying him about to dinners with friends or dinners alone and listening to his interminable stories about the film business fifty years ago and jokes which he remembered; the kind of jokes, I remembered, that my mother laughed at.

"I don't know what to do," I told Arieh when he called me after I returned home after these odd evenings. "I leave Alan alone all day and he can't really move about. I feel so sorry for him."

Arieh had taken to biking to make himself thinner. "I'll drop off a couple of papers for him at his hotel room when I go biking in the morning," Arieh said.

"That would be sweet."

"Maybe I'll take him to lunch," he added.

That was how it came about that as I went to meet Alan one day for lunch, I saw him sitting at a table mumbling, because he was losing his voice, with Arieh who suddenly looked stunned by the strength of his feelings for me as he watched me walk in the door.

"Did you tell Alan how much you love his films?" I asked Arieh as I sat down with them. After all, Alan was an icon of his, a film writer.

"Yes," he said gamely, "I did," but Alan said nothing and simply stared at me lovingly. He was seeing my mother.

I put my hand on Alan's, "Are you alright during the day all alone? Do you get any coffee?"

"I don't, I don't really remember," he chuckled, sweetly. "I'm a bit muddled, you know."

Arieh said he had to go off to a meeting and when he left the restaurant, Alan said, "He's a bit mad, isn't he?"

But I wasn't sure which one was mad. It struck me that they both were. Or maybe all people who are in love with phantoms or ghosts are mad. Meaning all of us.

Alan's visit upset me. I would go home and think why am I stuck with her boyfriend? And what does he want from me really?

My phone rang again.

"When can you look?" Joey said.

"I can't think about beds now," I said. "My mother's boyfriend is here and I am trying to avoid his asking me to get into his bed."

"How do you get yourself into these things?" he asked.

"I don't know. I really don't know."

The last night of Alan's visit I staged a huge dinner party at a restaurant with different friends to entertain him, to give Alan something festive. I wanted him to forget his grief. I wanted him to feel loved by me, even if it was platonic.

I invited Michael as my date.

I sat next to Alan and he kept putting his hand on mine. I pointed to Michael and said, "I think I like him."

Alan said, "He's a bit staid for you, isn't he? He's a type, you know. An English type. He looks like Alan Bennett."

I could never figure out if Alan was dotty or completely aware. It seemed to shift. He was dotty about his mistaking me for my mother. Or was he?

I ended up paying for this huge dinner for all my guests, as if I was rich, which I was not. Why was I doing this? Not to mention the thousands of taxis I took to get Alan and me around, even to get him across a street.

These taxis, rather than speeding me to my own world as they usually did, were wearing me down.

Alan left the next day for England, while I was working at my freelance job, and I wondered how he would manage the long walks at Heathrow Airport, "Get them to get you a chair at the gate," I said, and by the time he left, I remembered, I remembered how my mother's life had never really been good for me.

SEVENTEEN

A few days later, after yet another tedious, interminable day at that office where I struggled with technology writing of which I had absolutely no interest, nor the people who were developing it, nor the people who were supposed to buy it, all of which made Michael's money and willingness to take me away from it all the more attractive, I went home. I was lying on my couch, reading, at least happy to be in a world of my own making, when the phone rang.

I hoped it wasn't Alan. I just couldn't give out anymore.

"I am downstairs," Arieh said.

"Arieh, I have to work tomorrow. I have a freelance job where I have to be at the office. It's eleven at night. Alan wore me out."

"Just a few minutes. I want to give you something."

"Okay, I'll come down." I put on sandals and a dress and raced down to the gate in front of my building. If I brought him upstairs, I would never get rid of him.

He looked lonely standing there, with no one else on the street. His eyes didn't have their usual challenge.

He handed me a novel by Ouspensky. He loved it in his past, he said.

"Thank you," I said although I didn't much like the books he gave me. They were usually didactic rants, the one point in the book hammered ceaselessly, as he did in conversation.

"Alan is an anti-Semite, isn't he?" he said.

"Let's not get into that. He was a strain, I don't know about an anti-Semite."

"A narcissist, like your mother."

I nodded. I didn't say, we all are.

He held my hand.

"You are so beautiful," he said. "To me you are the most beautiful woman in the world."

I couldn't think why he kept saying this. Either he thought this bizarre thought because he is in love with me or it was a code to tell me he was in love with me.

"I want to take care of you. We'll laugh, we'll travel, you'll write. I can make enough money. We'll be happy. I am your mate," he said. I smiled sadly, thinking Yes, but do I want a domineering hysteric as my mate?

In response, I stroked the beige sweater, which covered his diminishing stomach, stroked it as if it was a Talmudic symbol I was paying homage to.

"How are you getting home?" I said to Arieh softly.

"I am walking. I like to walk, you know that."

"Yes."

"I am going away," I said, "in a week, to think."

"I'm not pushing you."

I gave him a look as if to say you must be joking.

"Well I don't like this hurting of everyone," I said.

He nodded.

"I don't know what to do."

Usually, he would have insulted me by now.

"I'm trying to figure this out," I continued.

"You love me," he said.

"Yes."

But I also love Michael, I didn't say. I'm not really going away for a week to think, I'm going away with Michael to see what I think about him.

"I will figure it out," I said.

EIGHTEEN

Before I left for my so-called holiday to "think," Arieh and I were walking together up Tenth Street to our weekly appointment with a shrink. I had agreed a month back to go to a shrink with Arieh to see how we could make him happier.

Arieh saw it as a way to get us more deeply embroiled. I saw it as a way to get us kindly and sanely dis-embroiled. Shows once again how stupid I was.

The shrink gave Arieh ideas on how to treat a woman. Compliment her. Buy her a gift. Don't criticize her. Accept her. Don't always think about yourself. Offer her a future. Support her.

These turned out to be very good ideas, because they were beginning to work. I started wondering if maybe Arieh really could be a husband, be a mate who would not destroy me.

It was a warm summer day as we were walking to our session, we both loved to walk, and he was in yet another expensive business suit, this time dark blue, with a red tie. He had become very sleek. Magically, he seemed to have transformed himself into the very man I wanted to be with. Elegant, smart, witty, strong.

Where was the fat, overbearing Arieh?

"I just brought in $10,000. For myself, I would have asked for $5,000 but now I am working for you," he said, "I doubled it and got it. You wouldn't need money if we were together. We would have one account."

"Really?" I asked, smiling.

"Yes," and then he pointed to a building that was under construction, a tall building overlooking a park we both liked. "We could get an apartment there," he said. "Shall we go in and look?"

"Not yet," I said.

He was not complaining about his life. He talked about a future. For the first time, it seemed he actually believed in something.

"It's funny, how we seem so compatible with each other," I said, walking next to him. I said this because we still spoke to each other extemporaneously, skipping about from subject to subject. I was fascinated by him.

"The Jews believe there is one person for you and you are that person for me. I am that person for you," he said.

I didn't want to do this and I didn't understand it at all but I found myself silently agreeing with him.

"Remember I told you I was going away?" I said as we continued walking to the shrink, "Well, I am. Soon."

"Oh really?" he asked, masking his feelings. "When?"

"Tomorrow."

"Why?"

"To think."

"Since when do you have the money to go away to think?"

"I'm going."

"Where?

"Sardinia."

"Sardinia? Oh come on. You must be going with this 'person' you're seeing."

"Okay, I am."

"Well don't."

"I said I would and so I am. Anyway I seem to be losing interest in him so maybe it's to end it. I don't know."

"Why are you telling me now?"

"I didn't tell you because I didn't want to upset your exams."

He looked at me. "Are you crazy?"

"I really think Arieh I am going to break up with him. It's not working. I'll, I'll come back to you."

We argued at the shrink and we argued after and, that night, as proof that I did love him, because I was beginning to think I did, I changed my behavior.

"Sleep with me," I said for the first time.

And we got into bed, and we kissed and we were close, so tied, so united and I brought him inside me and he didn't come. We were simply close.

"Why are you going with him?" Arieh kept asking me during the night.

"This will be the last time," I said. "I couldn't get out of it. I will let him down gently."

But he was right. Why was I going? It didn't make sense and yet I was reluctant to say no to Michael. I couldn't explain to Arieh that I wanted a last chance at a life that was not difficult.

I wanted to see if there was any possibility it might work with someone who had something to offer, someone with whom it was all seemingly effortless.

I didn't know then I simply might not love Michael. I thought I could force myself to, if I had to. I didn't know that you can't control love.

"Maybe it's indecision," I said.

"Indecision about what?"

I turned my back to him as we lay in bed. Indecision, I thought, about giving up quietude, a life of ease. Indecision about giving up what I thought would be a life of kindness with Michael. Maybe it was entirely different and it was indecision about Arieh, indecision about trusting my love for Arieh. Indecision about banking on happiness. Indecision about what was right and wrong for me or anyone else.

NINETEEN

Michael said, "Do you like it?"

He was referring to the hotel in Costa Smerelda we had just driven up to in a taxi with an older driver who looked more elegant than most of the businessmen in New York.

The hotel was whitewashed stone and Moroccan in design, and built in the nineteen-sixties by the Aga Khan. The Aga Khan's plan, Michael said, was to build low architectural designs that fit in with the Mediterranean landscape, thereby trumping the towering Hiltons. The Aga Khan made a lot of money with this plan, which he donated to a religious sect, he added.

I looked around the entry way and I felt a little drunk at the wild profusion of red flowers against all that white.

Sardinia.

When I was young and lived by the sea in a small rented apartment overlooking a rugged and sparkling cove—not as graceful as the one I was about to look out over—I read *Sea and Sardinia* by Lawrence. I saw in my mind rough-hewn people, an island that had never been conquered, soft mountains, ocean, wildness, truth.

In my forties, I read a biography of Beckett and I learned that he and his common-law wife, Suzanne, who played the piano, and whom he also cheated on, holidayed in Sardinia. Sardinia again.

When Michael said months ago, "Where shall we go?" I was a bit overtaken. No one had ever asked me "Where shall we go?" before. It seemed that my love life had been a continual managing of complaints. Mine or someone else's. I loved that Michael wanted to make our relationship work by doing nice things together.

I thought maybe this is the way. A sane man in exquisite places. It would be a marked change from a life of struggle and insecurity.

"It's beautiful," I said.

After we checked in, we walked along sparkling dark blue tile floors to an oval wooden door. Our room was pristine and large and I went right to the balcony windows.

The suite overlooked a green blue languorous bay, set like a sapphire emerald jewel amid the Sardinian mountains.

"It's just as exquisite as I'd imagined," I said to Michael, as I looked out through the long glass windows.

After Michael and I unpacked, we went to the bar, to see if having a drink might tire us enough to sleep. Michael had a Campari, as always. We sat and watched the handsome Italians. Men with full heads of dark hair, tall and slender in jeans, with sweaters crossed 'round their shoulders, moving quickly, almost effeminately, to cigarettes and girlfriends. They stood next to their seated tall young women in short and backless dresses who were speaking quickly to older women. The older women had completely effaced themselves from the sexual theatre, in bulky pants and loose jackets and frizzy hair, speaking in flat, deep voices. Some of the girls wore wide brimmed spring hats and tiny dresses that showed off their long tanned legs and Michael stared delightedly and I looked on sadly, as older women do.

I said, "I must get wireless."

We found out the wireless only worked in the lobby. We went back down to the lobby with my computer and Michael helped me sign up for an hour of wireless in Italian and I sent an email of love to Arieh. "Arrived this afternoon. Everything is always about you because you would love it here. Sardinia exquisite. Very windy and cool so no time outdoors yet. Miss you terribly and as of this minute I think we will have to be together. You and I have the electric energy. Romantically and even intellectually. I love you."

I ventured this, even with Michael sitting next to me, waiting to use my computer so he could check his own messages.

My passion for Arieh always seemed to catch fire when I was with Michael. I couldn't figure that out. Was Michael too like my father in his Englishness? Was it too Oedipal? Was Arieh so like my mother in her craziness and quixoticness that I had to be with him? The mother is always the beautiful one. This time the father will not win. This time I will be with my mother.

I finished writing my email and then passed the computer to Michael and he went on his email and noted that he had only received a few from list serves about rare books he had been searching for.

While he was checking, I imagined what it would have been like if I was there with Arieh. He would have been rushing about talking to the Italians in Italian, gossiping with the barman, finding out how to get to other parts of Sardinia, laughing, and generally having an enormously wonderful time.

That's what I imagined. Because, in truth, I never would have come to Sardinia with Arieh. He never would have given me such a gift.

Michael and I went into dinner. The restaurant was mostly empty since this; the last day of April, meant the summer season had not yet started. One couple sat near us, a blonde woman about my age whom you could tell had once been pretty but now was slightly overblown. She began to cry at dinner and, even before she did, I had noticed her husband being solicitous with her, trying to get her to eat. Either it was drink, I thought, or she has an illness she is facing. They left in the middle of their dinner.

I asked Michael when he began collecting Renaissance books.

"Ten years ago," he said.

Which is also the date he gave for when he began cheating on his wife, the date when he bought his house in the country, when he began to pay more attention to his business.

"Everything is ten years ago," I said. "Why?"

"I don't know."

"When did your father die?" I asked.

"About then," he said.

"Did he leave you the money to do new things?" I asked.

"Not really. Well, yes, I bought the house with that money."

"It's funny how people become more themselves when a parent dies."

Michael pointedly said nothing. He saw this line of conversation as American. The personal bored him yet he was choosing to write a novel. A novel of action, he called it.

He began reading the wine list.

I wanted to talk. I wanted to say people do become more themselves when their parent dies. My mother had recently died and here I was changing into someone I did not recognize. Someone who might have a happy future. Either with Arieh or Michael.

My mother had lived in nine different countries—Austria to Czechoslovakia to Palestine, while escaping Hitler, then Egypt to do her part for the British Air Force, then England, France, Canada, then back to England again.

"It's just another Jewish story," Arieh told me. "Jews always move around."

"Hitler's revenge," he added.

"What do you mean?"

"From everything you said she was mean and cruel to you."

"So?"

"She killed another Jew. You."

After dinner, Michael and I walked up the hotel steps to our room, past three pianos, and Michael took a sleeping pill because he slept badly even in normal times.

I said, "It's really beautiful here."

"I'm glad you like it," he said, and he smiled shyly.

I felt shy with him too.

I got into our hotel bed naked as I do, and Michael put on his pajamas, as he does, and we both fell asleep quietly in an unusually comfortable bed.

Two hours later we were awakened by a gunshot.

Ah Sardinia, island of pirates.

But soon the gun shots turned into a series of unremitting fireworks right outside our porch, very loud, and I wondered if it was for a marriage of one of the pretty Italian girls. Michael called the concierge in outrage but I knew it would end and so what? And he said in the morning it must have been for May Day.

TWENTY

After lunch the next day we lay by the pool, Michael under an umbrella to protect his delicate skin, and I in the sun to make havoc with mine, and a beautiful blonde in a thong bikini with long legs and flying hair was directly in front of us so Michael was distracted from reading Eco and giggled in a high pitch when she stood up with her well rounded bare buttocks facing him. I could not look at him; I did not want to see such desire mixed with embarrassment.

We came back to our room and worked a bit and then of course Michael wanted to make love. He is an older man, Michael, but not in the area of lovemaking. Maybe none of them are, I was discovering. Desire. So we did, but I was no longer in love; Arieh had hijacked me. I was missing him. I was missing how he would talk to me in bed; how he would make me laugh, make up any old story.

"Arieh is disturbed, you know," Michael had said at dinner, the night before.

"What made you think of Arieh?" I asked.

"I know how when you get distant, you're thinking about him."

I didn't deny it.

"I agree with you about his being disturbed," I lied, "but what makes you say that?"

"He's overreacted to your seeing someone else. His anger. His obsession to get you back. Why wasn't he with you in the first place? Then he asks you go into therapy with him. It's ridiculous. You shouldn't have done it."

"But I care for him."

Michael said nothing. Then, "Why?"

"He's emotional. He's suffered. Why should I just abandon him?"

Michael stared off.

"Don't you feel guilty," I asked, "that I am with you when he thinks you're his friend?"

"You say you didn't sleep together, you were always fighting. I gave him fifteen months to make something work with you. So it's really his own fault. I have no guilt," he said.

I nodded. There was something about the way Michael spoke that had the effect of shutting me down. Although I couldn't figure out what it was.

The next day when I went on wireless, there were two loving emails from Arieh. "Everything is strange because we're not together, and that is predictably and appropriately crazy making. I know where you belong: here, with me, loving, being loved, you know these things, don't be frightened. On the bike this morning I smiled at the thought that I went from being an unhappy Italian film star (in my mind) to a kind Italian film star (in my mind) in New York but you had to go to Italy. You needn't fear my love. I've learned well to be careful of you and to nurture you and stand back and see with boundless peace in my heart as you bloom."

Another one: "To quote someone I love more than anyone in the world, and more than I've ever loved anyone, I won't let anything bad happen to you."

He was quoting me.

Michael was sitting so close by, I could not reply freely. I could not understand why Michael sat so close to me when I received my emails. But then Michael stayed very close to me all the time, none of the usual thing with men where they want to go off to see this and that. No, Michael stayed next to me, hoping for female energy to revitalize him. I had been so touched by that at first that reverence. But now I reverted to wanting the friction that comes of the joining of male and female, that birth of one another, pushing each other, vehemently, bloodily, out of the canal, and not at all the civility I thought I wanted. It all made me sad and when I returned, I would return to Arieh for good.

That evening in Sardinia, Michael and I had a quiet dinner, talking a bit about language and Michael's belief that Shakespeare might have been the Earl of Oxford and what is it that is so marvelous about Tolstoy. Is plot important . . . no, no I said. But I don't know.

I slept fitfully, perhaps the Sardinian wine and the gunshots in my own mind. We woke again late, which is odd for me. I usually wake up early, even when jet lagged. I am always curious about the day.

But this unexpected lethargy was because we were locked away in this beautiful and secluded enclave. And the real Sardinians, swarthy and laughing, in old hotels and broken down piazzas and markets, were out there, gulping life, without me.

TWENTY-ONE

The next afternoon Michael and I took a taxi to a town close by, Porto Cervo, which Michael had seen on the map. "But everything is closed now," the concierge said, when we asked directions.

I became happy in the taxi as we took the hairpin turns that are the staple of Italy, an excursion, and I asked Michael, in French, if he was bored with me, seeing as he fell asleep in the afternoon and he was not tired.

"No I am not bored with you," he said, reaching for my knee. "You're being sensitive. I am extremely happy with you."

At that moment I thought I might be happy too. Being on the road in sea-wide Sardinia, with this gentle, polite Englishman who had brought me to this world of exquisite beauty and manners.

Michael once said to me, "I was born with a silver spoon."

I looked at him curiously.

"Well not really," he said. "My family was middle class but they gave me the best, as if I did have a silver spoon."

I said nothing but smiled.

It was such a sweet, amazing gift that he wanted to share his spoon with me.

On that afternoon drive, Sardinia was majestic at every turn. The ocean, the mountains, the light. I wondered if I could move here, to the capital, Cagliari, which we would not see, because it was too far south for a day trip. It made me a bit sad that my past lovers would have had us go anyway, would have forced us to push on, to see.

The next night at a quiet, empty restaurant with the Sardinian mountains hushed and soft in front of us, I said, "Alright. Zero to seven." I meant, tell me something about your past.

"Well I don't know why but I hardly remember my mother at all. Maybe she was too shy or retiring," he answered, uncomfortably.

"How old were you when she died?"

"It was only about 15 years ago," he said. Fifty. He was fifty when she died.

He looked away from me. He would prefer to talk ideas. But I feel ideas are born of psychological needs and byways.

It turned out, when I asked, he wasn't close to his father either.

"And you went off to boarding school at eight," I said, "with a stiff upper lip at five."

"Exactly," he said.

He was humoring me. He often told me his life was boring. Why did I want to talk about it, he asked?

"You know," I said, "I think your love life is the most interesting part of you."

"Why?"

"Well, your wives have been strong characters. A successful sculptor. A dress designer. Your mistresses, too. A pianist." I didn't want to include myself on the list because I was defecting.

"It's with women you took risks," I said.

"Moving to the States was a risk," he said. "I knew England was too provincial, too nineteenth century. I wanted the new."

And so do I, I felt. How could I possibly discuss anything with this man?

The conversation didn't lift. It didn't digress into humour, or exploration. It felt like summation.

In the night I couldn't sleep. Would Arieh wait for me, knowing I was in Italy with another man?

Finally, I drifted off, sad that I was there, seemingly alone in Sardinia, but in the middle of the night I was awakened by Michael punching his hands one against the other, as if he was fighting himself. Jacob and the Angel. I pulled his hands away from each other, thinking this was something he was doing in his sleep.

In the morning, I said to him, "Did you know you were punching your hands against each other in your sleep?"

"Oh yes," he said in British. "It's a type of exercise."

I felt so lonely in Sardinia with Michael. So lonely with this silence. Or was it being with myself? So lonely in this affluence without any conflict.

The next night, I wrote Arieh. I said, "Start making plans. We are going to get married."

TWENTY-TWO

Michael had a surprise for us, he said, after Sardinia. We were going to Como. He wanted to buy an apartment over the lake. A home. I thought, I'll go along with it and he will enjoy this place with someone else. I am looking at houses for her.

As we drove to the airport to fly to Milan, I felt secure with him. Not to mention, the world was now full of amazing surprises. When did I ever think I would travel to Como? I felt that I was learning new things that were not part of my previous life of being land-locked, thinking up incessant ways to pay the rent. I was seeing a softer, gentler, more exquisite life. I couldn't be part of it, because I did not love Michael in the right way, but we were friendly and this was an enormous bounty to be treated well.

"You'll see," he said, "the *lago* is one of the most beautiful places in the world. I always wanted to have a place there."

At first, as we drove in from Milan, Como seemed dingy, but as we got closer, I saw that Como is sonorous, understated, a bastion of medieval secrets. I saw tiny streets with gates along the road and, behind them, piazzas and flowers and above them sober apartments with long windows and shutters. I saw that the town is lodged in a crevice among the mountains; the town has the same somber, deep aesthetic as listening to a bassoon.

Our hotel was built in the 12th Century and we had a room with a canopied bed. The owner, behind the desk, had longish grey hair and glasses, piercing intelligent eyes, as if he read constantly and listened to music. He wore a brown corduroy suit and had an elegant deep voice. I wondered what it would be like to live with a man so seemingly ensconced in a life of beauty and simplicity.

At night, Michael and I walked to the empty old part of Como for dinner. "Why are there so many shops for women's clothes?" he asked.

"So we can attract you people."

But it was the conversation that got me down. It seemed as if I was acting. I heard myself: "So we can attract you people." Whose voice was that?

I longed for Arieh and our unexpected digressions. Only four more days till I got back and I would be my old creative spontaneous self.

I had emailed Arieh that. "Only four more days," I wrote.

The old town of Como was mostly stone, exquisitely kept up, and we found a small restaurant next to a miniature Vatican and a large concert house. The restaurant seemed to be where people in the theatre went. There were pictures of actors and actresses all over the walls. I had a veal chop, unheard of for me since I usually eat vegetables, and it was so good I began gnawing at the bones for more meat as if I was a dog.

Michael got a piece of paper and worked out the numbers of the house over the lake we had looked at during the day. I was shocked at this kind of affluence but enjoyed masquerading as a woman of means. It was probably the last time in my life I would ever do that.

The Swiss chalet he looked at was perfectly kept with gleaming wood floors and huge picture windows, with a large porch over the mouth of Lake Como.

The snow peaked mountains were both soft and powerful surrounding the tranquil lake.

But Michael was not sure about the place. He said it would be boring to have to deal with the extra land that came with the house.

I couldn't understand what would be boring about it. It seemed like a bonus to me. Or he could sell it.

"But," I said, "you need a project. What do you want for the next few years?"

"To stop working," he said. "And just jet set."

He was vague.

He looked at me longingly, hoping that it would be me who would increase the elan in his life. This is what women do, I realized, for some rich men.

I looked away.

"What do you want?" he asked.

"To write," I said. "I don't know."

It was dawning on me how tense he was. He never just sat back and joked.

Arieh would say it was because he was not Jewish.

Arieh once said to me, "Michael's a bit of a drip, isn't he?"

The unfortunate sentence never left my mind.

I looked over at Michael and I could not understand why he was so unhappy and harried, sitting there silently and glumly. Here we were, doing the most joyful of things—looking at a house overlooking Lake Como.

I wanted to cry. But the truth is obvious: it was I who was unhappy, ascribing it to him. This was a dream come true, this kind man and a house in Como, and here I was, thinking I must get away.

TWENTY-THREE

The night Michael and I arrived back in New York, Arieh was sitting long-legged in a suit and blue shirt, waiting for me at an outdoor bar on 7th Avenue. I could see, immediately, I was in for trouble. He seemed all angles and taut like a panther about to unfurl for attack.

I motioned that we should go downstairs where there is a fireplace. Two models were sitting next to us with their incomparably long legs and pulled back hair. They were busy talking about boyfriends and saw no one but each other.

He lunged into the chair. I sat gingerly, waiting for the upcoming onslaught.

"You are well, I trust?" he asked somewhat sarcastically.

"Alright."

I had not kissed him when I saw him. I had not yet shifted from being on a plane with Michael two hours ago to the reality of now sitting in a restaurant with Arieh. I had told Michael on the plane that he and I had difficulties in our relationship, but Michael and I came to no conclusion. I didn't have the heart.

"Good trip?" Arieh asked.

"Yes." I looked at him sadly, mutely.

"Do you love me?"

"Yes," I said. I did love him. But looking at him, at his masked face and taunting eyes, I did not know what I loved.

"Are you finished with your new boyfriend whose name I learned is Michael. Michael, my friend."

"Oh. So you know."

"Yes of course I know. Thank you for telling me," he said sarcastically. "Let me tell you it wasn't very difficult to figure out. Naturally you didn't tell me the truth. You knew it was wrong. Sleeping with my client, my friend of fifteen years. Not something you'd want to be too open about."

I listened.

"You know how I found out? His office said he was away. Curious, I thought. I called his daughter and she gave me the name of the hotel in Sardinia. There you were. Both registered. I wanted to tell you both to fuck off but friends told me not to."

I nodded.

"He is nothing sleeping with my girlfriend," he continued.

"I wasn't your girlfriend."

He ignored that. "At first I thought I couldn't compete. He's high born. Then I realized he has no feelings."

"That's not true. Anyway, I will stop this duplicity," I said. "I promise that."

"When?"

"Now. Not tonight," I said. "I am tired. I just arrived."

"You are incapable of stopping anything," he said.

"Were you fucking him while you were writing me loving emails?"

"I don't need to answer that," I said.

"Are you trying to hurt me?" he asked.

"No."

"You lie," he said. "You lie to me. You deserve each other, you're both liars and worthless. I am sick of you."

"Okay," I said.

His voice had changed to a higher register; his face was cold and bitter. "You are nothing," he said to me, "sleeping with him while loving me. Why did you write me those emails? Why did you say you loved me and you were fucking him? My client? My friend who turns on me. You just used me. I was your toy while you were bored with Michael. You come home and nothing has changed. You will never make up your mind. You can't. You don't know how to love.

"You are a whore," he spat out. "A whore. You're both nothing," he continued.

The couches and fireplace and bar music were starting to spin around me.

I pleaded mildly. "I have been trying to work this out. You didn't want me and I got into this and I am trying to understand it. It took time."

"Not this much. You don't know how to love. I thought you were coming back to me."

"I was, am. But I need to tell him—"

"I thought you were going to tell him in Italy."

"I did. I told him it wasn't working. I was depressed with him."

But Arieh was right. I had not been clear. I had been duplicitous.

We always were in accord about this one thing. I was wrong.

Finally tired and feeling as worthless as he intended me to, I said, "I must go home." He followed me along the street, continuing on with how I hurt him, and I listened, almost numb from his barrage.

I have to end it with Arieh, I told myself. He is impossible. I loved him. I loved him because he had talked so much of love and his need for me. I had loved that.

But we can't, we can't be safe together.

Later that night Arieh called me. I was sitting at my desk, as I always am when I am home.

"I leveled the playing field," he said. His voice was high and excited.

"Yes?"

"I forwarded all your emails of love to me to your boyfriend."

I hung up and cried. I hated that he had taken something between us and treated it as public domain. I hated that he had hurt Michael, who, in my opinion, was an innocent bystander.

I hung up and went to my crumpled, mixed up bed and didn't answer the phone the next 20 times it rang from Arieh who left messages that I had hurt him and now he had hurt me.

TWENTY-FOUR

"I guess that's that then," Michael said, when he called at 7 a.m. the next morning.

"Well, no."

"It isn't?"

Michael was a businessman. He was going to let me talk, let me hang myself.

"No. We should speak in person," I said. "We should go over this together," even though I didn't know what I was going to say.

At noon, he came over and I paced between my two couches. I didn't wonder at the time why he didn't just finish with me.

But, in a way I understood. He had used many of the same idioms about women that my father had. Women are fundamentally crazy, my father would say. Michael had used those very same words about his wife: she's crazy. Women are illogical, sources of trouble, my father said. Women are untrustworthy and unreliable. I had heard Michael say those traits came with the territory of women. Men just end up loving us anyway. It was taken for granted that we're minefields. It's part of our beauty.

Really? I thought. No wonder I couldn't commit to anyone.

That said, Michael took it upon himself to come up with a reason about why I had maintained contact with Arieh. "Well you really had no proof I would leave my wife, so you probably were hedging your bets."

We went out to lunch downstairs on Second Avenue. It was an Italian restaurant, the same one where I had talked to Arieh on a cellphone when I was waiting for Michael to pick me up in a car to take us to Sardinia.

The sun was warm on us. The cars raced by noisily.

"My wife is so anxious to get rid of me," he said drily as he sat down, "that she is circling apartment listings for me."

Why is it me who gets stuck with him? I thought. She is probably tired of the ponderous silence also.

I made calls to realtors for him on my cellphone as we ordered off the menu.

Not a moment soon enough, he headed back uptown to the wife who was trying to get rid of him.

At five in the morning Arieh called me.

I listened, breathing shallowly. I kicked a morass of covers that were all over the bed away from me, looked for a pillow and found one on the floor.

"I don't want to talk about this," I said. "I no longer love you. You killed it by sending those emails."

"I brought everything to the surface."

"You took something that was private and what you did was vicious. I don't want to see you or talk to you." I hung up.

He called back 15 times and either I didn't pick up or I pressed talk and then end or sometimes I screamed at him and said, "It's over. We are finished. We are too destructive."

"You can get Michael back," he said. "Let him fight for you if he so loves you just as I did for six months and got nowhere. Let him fight for you."

I hung up.

The next day, Michael decided to visit me again after his looking at apartments. Obviously, he had taken to keeping an eye on me. I had the feeling he thought that my errant behavior was because he had not been around enough. I was too weak to be left alone. Now, he wanted to drop by all the time.

He sat on the couch across from me and he told me that none of the apartments he had seen that day were right. To prove it, he showed me some layouts and said, "I don't know where we would put a room for you in this place."

I nodded, relieved. I was going to have to tell him: I couldn't possibly move in with him. My infatuation had ended. Even though I didn't want it to. I would have had such a pleasant life with him. But it had gone. Gone to some place where I couldn't find it.

"Also," he said, "I think it's better if we live on the Upper East Side. This neighborhood of yours is too young."

I loved this neighborhood of mine, even if it was full of NYU students and I was the oldest person in the Village. I loved the businesses that were not chains; I loved the fact that the area was not about money. It was writers and painters and immigrants and students.

I didn't say anything because I knew in my heart he would be looking for an apartment alone, even though he didn't realize it yet.

"Aren't you angry at me," I asked, "for my deceptions?"

"I think you just need support," he said. "I think you just need to be treated well."

I looked at him, confounded.

"Have you heard from Arieh?" he asked.

"Yes, but we are trying not to speak to each other," I said.

TWENTY-FIVE

But neither Arieh nor I were good at not speaking to each other. We called each other incessantly. The more we agreed to never speak again, the more in touch we were.

I called him the next night the minute I got home from dinner with a friend.

"I've just got in from shul," he said. "I've decided. I am finished. I will have no more contact with you. I cannot go on like this. I should have done this," he said, "months ago."

I agreed. Why should he continue to call me? I am a terrible person. No wonder he hates me. Or loves to hate me. Or whatever it is. I deserve nothing.

We were silent for a few seconds.

Then I asked, "What is your father like?"

"A sadistic hysteric," he said.

We were both silent for another few seconds.

Then he said, "And you are like your lying mother."

The next night I was almost feverish.

I called Arieh at two in the morning, "Let me stay with you one last night."

"Yes," he said. "Do that. Let's have a goodbye party."

It was only a few minutes before I was walking through his small lobby with a chandelier and flowers on the table. The doorman was asleep, with his head down on the entryway desk.

I got on the elevator, went to the third floor, and rang the buzzer. Arieh opened the door in his old, rumpled dressing gown. As black as our behavior was, we smiled when we saw each other. We walked to his bedroom and he pulled my dress over me as we reached his bed. We immediately fell on the bed and began to make love. Naturally, with his personality, he was rough. He pulled my legs over my head. He pinched my nipples. He kissed my eyes, my lips. He bit my ear. I pulled away. He became a little more gentle and we made love for a short distracted time and then I felt that old sadness that I feel with everyone, and I said, "Let's go to sleep. I must go to sleep." And then we slept spooned up together, me in his big hairy body which I loved.

He held me. I held him.

In the morning, Arieh said, "I am your slave. I will do anything you ask me to. I am your eunuch."

"You should just piss on me," he said. "It would be more honest."

He was frightening me by talking like this.

"No," I said. "Let's do what you said and separate and I will go through what I have to go through and then we will see."

He got on top of me and entered me and he said, "What do you want me to do? Tell your slave what you want."

"Come inside of me," I said.

And he did.

Then we held each other.

"It's important, you know," I said, meaning coming inside.

"I know."

"I must get up," I continued. "I am losing my business. I am completely losing everything."

He said, "Me too. I have done the same."

"Then," I said, zipping up my dress, "we must go back to work and get our lives in order." I looked around for my sandals.

"I won't call you," he said.

"I know," I said. "It will kill me."

At the door, Arieh said, "Have a good time with Michael."

I said, "Don't say that."

He handed me a bag he had for me of two law transcripts that he said would show me both his brilliance and aggressiveness, another book by Kenneth Burke ("Am I smart enough to read this?" I asked. "Yes," he said), the Psalms and some of his own writings.

I took them.

He was handsome to me standing at the door, tall with his long fingers. My father also was tall and had long fingers. My father also chose badly in women. My father destroyed the women who married him. He was autocratic, unforgiving, verbally abusive. After all, he was a drunk. Women never existed in their own right for him. My Jewish mother was intelligent enough to run away. And dead enough inside to leave me with him.

Did I hate them all?

When I got home from being with Arieh, I told myself in the bathtub: Countless people have gone through this breaking up with someone with whom they had a tempestuous relationship. I told myself this. This is normal.

TWENTY-SIX

The next night, I followed Arieh to the Turkish restaurant. I was pretty sure he would be there, for that was what he did, ate alone in restaurants, with the New York Post and an uneasy rapport with the waiter. I rushed in, nervous, hurting, looking around desperately, and there he was, sitting solitary at a table, his napkin tucked into his shirt, eating fish on the bone, with a bottle of wine.

He looked up at me as if it was completely natural that I should walk in.

"I admire your Napoleonic moves," he said, as I silently sat down. This compulsion to see him, to find him, was overpowering me. I must be with him, I cried inside. He can't throw me away. We are tied by invisible threads of iron. Doesn't he know?

"You don't look very good," he said.

He was referring to how haggard I had become. This yearning for kindness from him.

"Napoleon said the war is not over till he declared it over," Arieh said.

I nodded.

"You know what Hitler, Stalin and Napoleon had in common?" he continued.

"No."

"Where was Napoleon born?"

"Corsica. Hitler was Austrian. Stalin?" I asked.

"Georgian. None of them were born in the countries they led," he said.

I nodded, a bit dazed. I hated these quizzes. Language quizzes. History quizzes. What relevance did they have? It astounded me that he ordered a full bottle of wine just for himself. I had a few sips.

It didn't astound me, it worried me.

"I will never forgive you," he said, spearing his fish and looking back down to the Post. "Be with Michael."

I said nothing. I believed that those sentences, which he repeated over and over, were some kind of mantra to ensure he wouldn't be vulnerable with me. I didn't know they were another cross dress. Those words and his rage and his refusal to forgive were how he merged with his mother in Auschwitz, fighting the enemy. We must all be punished.

I believed I simply had to wait for him to get sick of these accusatory sentences. I was sure eventually he would. Love is stronger than hate, isn't it?

I wasn't looking at what was behind the sentences.

"Are you familiar with Herod?" I asked, knowing that Herod beheaded his favorite wife whom he believed to be unfaithful to him. Beheaded her entire family too. Only Salome, her daughter, survived.

"He was a sonofabitch," he said.

Like you, I thought.

"You don't understand, do you," he said, "what you have done? You fucked my friend. You betrayed me when I loved you. You are a monster with no feelings. I can never get over it. I didn't need this at my age. I didn't need to be destroyed by your silly games."

Then he changed tack.

"Want to go watch a movie?" he asked. "Let's go watch *Marnie*, a movie about you. About a liar and sick woman whom Sean Connery loves."

We rented it with my credit card. Apparently he had some complicated situation going on with payment at the video store and I also had noticed that his home phone had been shut off too. Go to Michael, he always said. At least you'll have money.

We got into his messy huge bed to watch the film.

"Take off your clothes," he said. "They'll get crumpled in the bed."

That was true. And I was trying to get close to him. I'll be like the Poles, when they wanted freedom, they just acted free. I will act like we are a couple. I took off my clothes and put my head on his enormous chest, and he put his arm around me, and this gave me a little hope.

In the film, Sean Connery is kind to his mentally deranged wife, tries to help her figure out what happened to cause her such pain that she steals, lies, cannot get close to a man.

The only thing Tippi Hedron, his wife, loves are horses and Sean buys her a horse to show her some love, to try to soften her.

"That's sweet," I said, when I saw Sean drive up to the house with a horse trailer.

At that Arieh slapped me across the face. It didn't hurt but the humiliation did. "Something Michael would do," he said meaning buy the horses.

I slunk to the other side of the bed and began dressing to go home. He pulled my bra away from me and threw it across the room.

I was almost too tired to leave and, for some reason, I wanted to see the end of the movie.

I sat away from him, on the bed, with my knees up to my chest, facing the television.

Arieh is ill. I am ill to want him so. I should want Michael, just as Arieh says.

But Michael is boring. Or is he? What can I tell about anyone, I said to myself, right now. I am out of my mind.

After the movie ended, I said to Arieh, "I liked it. Sean was a lot nicer to her than you are to me."

"She didn't fuck his friend."

I couldn't argue with that. But I was too tired to say what I realized the next morning was the perfect response, "She stole his money." My taking $20 from Arieh would have put him over the edge. He was not a generous man. Except about meals. He would buy you food at any time of day or night.

In the morning Arieh wanted to make love.

"I don't fuck people who slap me," I said. "Let me sleep."

He kept trying.

"Suck my dick."

"No."

"Spread your legs."

"No."

Finally he let me sleep a bit and then began trying again.

"You need a blow up doll," I said, "with many orifices."

"I have one, you."

"Be nice for 60 seconds and maybe we can make love," I said.

For 60 seconds he held me and told me he loved me.

"60 seconds are up," he said, and then he pushed himself inside me. I could not kiss him; I was too tired, and too hurt by him. But I began to like the feel of him. "Kiss me," he kept saying and I couldn't. But I could fuck him and he said, "I want to come inside you," and I did want that, "Okay come inside me, I want you to come inside me," I whispered and at that he did.

I held him.

And then got up.

"You know we can't be together," he said. "We're both too crazy. I will never forgive you. And I will always hit you like that."

I climbed over him and just kissed him softly. Maybe I could congeal him together. He was so broken apart.

"Want to have breakfast," he asked, "with Sol?" His eighty-year-old lawyer friend.

"No," I said. "I look too strange. I don't have a toothbrush here, and I have to go."

"You look fine."

"No."

"Then go, get out of my life," he said.

And I left his apartment, shutting the door not sure what had just happened.

Later that night, he called me and said, "Come over."

"No," I said.

"I saw last night," he said, "that you are haunted. I am destroying you. But it's a good thing."

I said nothing. What was this? It reminded me of Moses throwing God's tablets down in anger when he saw that the Jewish people were worshipping idols while he was up there conversing with God. When he came back down from the mount, Moses threw a tantrum he did not feel to prove his point to his people. They were liars, infidels, betraying God like that. Moses feigned fury, trying to shock them back to their senses. In reality, he allegedly felt compassion for them.

Arieh continued on the phone, "All that charm and cuteness had to be destroyed. Now you will be your real self."

I sighed.

"You fell in love with that charm and cuteness you are so willing to rip out of me," I said.

"No you were quiet the first few times I met you. I've destroyed what had to be destroyed."

I began to cry as he said this. Cry, for how alone I had always been. What was being destroyed bit by bit was my belief that I could have a normal life. I was letting it go. As I maybe had destroyed it for him when I slept with his friend and now he had destroyed it for me with his anger and chaotic hell that he hurled at me whenever he could.

I don't remember hanging up the phone that night.

"Now," he said, "you can love someone."

TWENTY-SEVEN

Michael kept calling me, while I was losing my mind. "Let's get together," he said, even though I had turned my attention completely away from him. But he wasn't guilty of any crimes, not like Arieh and me, so I felt I should maintain friendly contact. I knew I couldn't see him clearly anymore, now that I was blinded by obsession for Arieh.

Arieh didn't feel the same way. To him, Michael was not innocent at all. Arieh hated him. "How can he have gone after you, when he was my friend? Why didn't he tell me he wanted to go out with you? That's what a decent person would do."

"People are not perfect," I said.

"He is a piece of shit," Arieh said. "He was no friend to me. He was just my client, trying to get my services cheap. He didn't care a whit about me. Neither of you did. He probably hates Jews, like all the Brits."

"That's not true at all," I said, although I had noticed how Michael expressed dismay about my growing interest in the Jewish side of my background.

"Why are you looking into it?" Michael asked.

"Why shouldn't I?" I said.

If I can't have a mother, let me have the God of her ancestry.

I went to visit Michael one Sunday afternoon. He did not instantly insult me as I walked through the door. This was a welcome change. "What would you like to do this afternoon?" he asked as we sat down to talk.

I was struck by how pretty and comfortable and orderly his apartment was. The bathrooms were clean. The windows looked out over a quiet 88th Street with its doormen, elegant doorways and well-behaved children. The world was not asunder here.

"Let's just stay in your apartment," I said.

"Why?" he asked. "It's beautiful out. Let's walk around the reservoir. The entire park is in full bloom. It's gorgeous."

"Alright," I said. I saw his point. I couldn't hide here, even though I wanted to. What kind of coward was I?

"You have to stop talking to Arieh," Michael said as we walked once again 'round the reservoir. "It is ruining you." I had taken to wearing large sunglasses because my face was so drawn and sad from continually being told by Arieh how terrible I was. It seemed to be having a physical effect on me.

"You're a wonderful person," Michael said. "I'm not going to let him destroy us."

Us. Michael still thought of us as a couple. He did not pay attention to the fact we hadn't slept together in ages, that I was never available. He was willing our relationship into existence.

"It's my fault really," he said.

"Why?" I asked.

"I should have taken you off to Argentina or got you out of here and away. We should have gone anywhere together where he couldn't get to you."

"Anna Karenina," I said and smiled without mirth.

I didn't like that his solutions always seemed to be a total capture of me, Michael and I alone in the world. He, sweeping me away.

Didn't he know the madness was inside me? Not in Arieh?

"Is he still suing you?" I asked, to change the subject.

"He is. He has a lawyer who is as crazy as he is. His lawyer screams at my lawyer. Can you imagine?"

"What is he suing you for?"

"He says I owe him back money."

"Do you?"

"I don't want to discuss it with you," he said.

"He tells me," I said, "that he wants to subpoena me. But what do I have to do with your owing him or not owing him money?"

"He's mad," Michael said.

"I know," I said, but I couldn't admit that I was crazy too, that nothing, no matter how bad it was, was stopping me from getting in touch with Arieh. I seemed to be addicted to the rush of his rejection. He'd pull toward me with a battery of calls, and maybe even a pleasant dinner, and then he'd abruptly and violently pull away. Wouldn't speak to me. If I called him to find out why not, he'd tell me he was too busy. "Come on, come on," he'd say abruptly, as if I was an annoyance. Finally, he'd blurt out, "I don't want to be with someone as evil as you."

The whole effect created a physiological craving in me. I am a good person, I'd tell myself. You must see it, my mind screamed.

"You have to put down the phone when he calls," Michael said, sadly, knowing that his words were words to the wind.

"I love you," Michael continued. "I want us to have a decent life and you insist on this destruction of yourself. You're sensitive. Intelligent. And this whole thing is taking you away from yourself."

I nodded.

But even listening to all this, my body was craving the pain of Arieh.

I left Michael that afternoon, and took myself to an early Woody Allen film, *Manhattan*. I was older than most of the audience and it occurred to me these people had never seen the film when it came out. They were in strollers when Woody was showing his persona overcome with feelings.

And that smart Jewish wisecracking neurotic sweet man on the screen was the Arieh I had fallen in love with. It was just that my particular smart Jewish wisecracking neurotic man was not the man on the screen at all.

"His not forgiving you is a Jewish thing," a friend said who lived downstairs as we shared one of her cigarettes. "There must be justice. He must make you pay. Otherwise, the Nazis will take over. That's why he's always saying you must pay the consequences."

Well, I had paid enough consequences. *Genug ist genug.* I would get out of it now. I had survived a drunk father, an abandoning mother. Or at least I had tried to. What I hadn't survived was the way I treated myself. No child. No marriage. No career. No education. And then came a man who smashed into my face that I had not treated him as valuable either. Alright. I saw. I saw that I had been a liar with men. I saw that I had not believed in love for myself. I saw that my first instinct was to throw myself away. And anyone who wanted to be with me.

I better, just in gratitude for having been given life, start to change all this.

I just had no idea how.

TWENTY-EIGHT

As if he heard my thinking, Arieh suddenly changed. No more nastiness. No more attacks. He began to call all the time. "How are you?" "What are you doing?" His voice was gentle, loving. "Are you alright?" "Do you want to have dinner tonight?"

Then he'd begin a litany. "In a few moments, I am off to court, then I'm going to my office to finish my billing. Then to Dr. Leli, then to shul."

"Okay," I said, not knowing why he was suddenly treating me as if I needed to know his every whereabout. Well, I did know why. He wanted to feel connected. We all do.

He began going to a shrink four days a week. To recover from his anger.

"What are you doing?" he asked me, when he called.

"I am off to a concert, after I finish trying to find work."

Sometimes he called seven times a day.

I thought it odd but I tried not to be attached to it. Alan no longer called obsessively. He was now living with nurses and I guess otherwise distracted, so it was only Arieh who broke my solitary silence at my desk.

I kept myself busy with friends, with films, music, books. I would only see Arieh if I had nothing else to do. I couldn't risk his turning on me, although he seemed to have stopped doing that on the phone. But what would he do if I needed him or if I was vulnerable to him?

And I was beginning to have whole sets of hours when I did not think about him, whole sets of hours when I did not hate myself.

The nights, however, in my bed were another matter. I would awaken at three in the morning, worried. Rather than feeling I had to be with Arieh, I began to feel I had to find a way to take care of myself. The economy was shot and I was older, and recently broken inside. Who would hire me? I saw that I was ill prepared for a future, and I began to wonder if part of my obsession with him had been to not look at the fact that work was becoming harder to find, and that I was alone.

"I can't make ends meet," I would tell him on the phone, as I was walking to the gym. "I had this breakdown with you. And then I ruined my life by not taking care of myself to begin with. I have thrown myself away."

"What do you think I have done?" he said. "I don't make any money either."

"But you're a lawyer. You bill in an hour what I make in a day."

"What makes you think I get paid?"

I sighed. "Why is it I am telling you that I am having a hard time and we're talking about you?"

But I knew. I knew he was telling me he could not take care of me.

He said on the phone, "Teach. Advertise to teach."

Since he was the one I talked to so much, I listened to him.

I placed ads. I tried. I got a few students but not enough to live on.

"Be yourself," he said. "You're talented and smart. You'll find something."

Occasionally he sent me $300 or so in the mail. It was sweet.

"Bank it," he'd say, when I called to ask why he had sent it.

If I did see Arieh for dinner, I listened to his tales of Paris and Amsterdam, to his complaints about work and then I used the excuse of his messy apartment not to sleep over. "I am not staying there anymore. It's not healthy."

"You're right," he said. "No one should."

"Why don't you get a cleaning lady?"

"I'm not ready," he said.

I knew that the horror of his apartment was to keep us all away.

I didn't invite him to sleep at my place either. We were frightened to get involved after what had ensued. We could not leave each other and could not be with each other. We had lived through a searing of our souls together, and we had not abandoned each other—we even loved each other for catalyzing this burning of ourselves into reality. We both now were in life, not running from it, and we were both trying to rebuild ourselves.

"You know the children who survived Auschwitz the best," he said, "were the ones who had their mothers with them."

I looked out the window, as he said this. I saw all our grief. His. Mine. All our relatives. All of us. This is what he brought me. A holding note of grief.

I had needed to feel it. For not having a mother. And for my mother not having a mother. Arieh had given me that.

But I didn't want that to be the sum total of my life.

"I don't understand why you don't want to be in a relationship," I'd say. "I don't seem to want to be alone anymore. I used to. But now, now I want someone there. I am not furious with rage anymore."

"It's because of me," he said, "that you don't want to be alone anymore."

And maybe that was true. I had had to confront myself with him. The messiness of it, all that need that welled up in me. It had nearly killed me but not sublimating those needs had freed me to be real, to desire.

"Well how come you don't want to be together?" I asked.

He'd answer, "I'm exhausted."

I knew what he meant. He was exhausted trying to heal himself from a life alone.

I was exhausted, too.

All I had was Judaism.

I took Torah classes each week and listened. I gleaned a little about what a moral life was. I sat around a table in the basement of a synagogue and listened with another spinster and a younger man who had trouble reading. We listened to the wiry, excitable Rabbi explain why God came up with such bad ideas as suggesting that his people make cattle and lamb offerings to please Him.

"It's cruel," we said.

The Rabbi agreed and explained God was transitioning Pagan rituals to His time.

I took a class on the Talmud and loved the intellectual young Rabbi's stories of yeshiva students who love God too passionately or did not love God passionately enough. God always teaches them a lesson, like a Zen master. It turned out that God wants us to live this life, now; He is ultimately practical. Now, He says.

I took a class on Nietzsche and Judaism and bathed myself in Nietzsche's belief in overcoming.

Every story was about suffering. Every story had hope.

And the Jews. The Jews were the only people I felt safe with. They knew that you shored yourself up against the travails of life by working, by bonding together.

I had done neither of those well but I watched and learned.

Arieh sometimes waited for me outside my class. He would be standing outside by a tree on the sidewalk, and we would turn silently toward a local hotel where the bar had a fireplace and those big armchairs that one imagines belonging in a British country house and he would walk very slowly, for he was always uncomfortable with his huge body. He'd become fat again. He'd pour his wide self into a chair by the fire and have a long discussion with the waitress about dessert wines. Then he'd ask me what I had learned in class. Like a child, I would tell him.

He'd correct my Hebrew. "Did the Rabbi say," he'd ask, "what Moses said when he saw them with the Golden Calf?"

Then Arieh would begin speaking Hebrew to himself.

I'd listen. He'd translate. Now his repetitions were Hebrew sayings, not how terrible I was. He'd pull out of his pocket a book for me. *Laughter* by Henri Bergson. I could not think why.

I'd rub his stomach affectionately for just how fond I was of him and then we'd get up and leave and he'd walk me to the corner of Lexington and I'd flag a cab.

"Why can't you take a bus?" he asked. "You're a poor woman."

I'd shrug, then smile like a naughty child as I swung my legs into the cab, and not say what I was thinking: the last thing I want to feel, ever feel, is that I am a poor woman.

Did he sleep with men? Did he not want anyone? I didn't know.

"My life is finished. My life is ended," he said, when I told him this was not natural. People pair up.

"What do you mean by together?" he'd ask. "You mean having breakfasts and lunches together and so on?"

It seems he saw everything in meals.

I nodded.

"It's too late for me," he said.

Michael still called me. He was seeing women but he never seemed to like them much. Was it possible he really loved me?

I told Michael I was having trouble making a living so he hired me one day a week to work for him so I would have some money.

On the days I was there I sat next to him at his long desk in his office at my own computer and we worked companionably together, as I looked over the Central Park trees and Park Avenue and the city from his high-rise glass apartment. We chatted about mutual friends. About his family. About books. We laughed. He spoke to brokers about his investments.

He played the piano for me. I edited his essays on renaissance emblems.

"Come to Italy with me," he said. "I will cover your expenses while we're away."

I shook my head.

"Why not?" he said.

I didn't know.

I was going to have to be Jewish, I realized, and choose a man. The Rabbi had said in one of our Torah classes, as we left, "May you marry the one you love."

A blessing.

I looked imploringly at Michael.

"I don't know."

TWENTY-NINE

If I don't want to be alone, then do something about it, I told myself. I decided to try online dating to meet a man. Suddenly a profusion of men appeared. Short ones. Educated ones. Successful ones. Self impressed ones. Kind ones. Angry ones. All wanting to be loved, to be found, to be healed from divorces, children growing up, young women not willing to commit.

I began going on numerous dates. Concerts. Dinners. Lunches. Some of these were boring, some were not. Sometimes

I slept with one, to force myself to not live off phone calls. To teach myself that a real body was better. Arieh had taught me to stay away. Just stay away. It was amazing to be in someone's arms again. To be held. To find someone nice to me in the morning.

And then I would lose interest. They either didn't really want to communicate or I realized I had nothing in common with them or they suddenly had a girlfriend they had not mentioned.

But it changed me.

It reminded me that this is what men and women do. They get together. These men did seem to want to be with a woman. They were willing.

I was trying to change my internal chemistry by remembering, remembering that love involves proximity.

Arieh did not seem to mind that I was otherwise engaged. Or he acted like he didn't. If he caught me in a mood where I wanted emotional contact with him, he'd say, "Let me grow up a bit." "After I finish this case." "I am trying to catch up after ruining my life."

The secret for decent relations with him was to want nothing. That was the same secret for good relations with my mother.

As I was musing thus, the buzzer rang. Arieh hated my stairs so I was pretty sure it wasn't him.

"Okay look at this," Joey said, as he barged in as if war had been declared on the East Village. He was carrying a Macy's catalog. "There's a sale. You're too nuts to go look at a bed. Just order this one. It's perfect."

I took the catalog out of his hands. The bed was pretty, a four-poster. Substantial and light.

"Okay."

I went to the phone, called Macy's and gave them my credit card number.

"That was easy," I said. "What took me so long?"

"Jesus," Joey said, "next thing you know you may even get a metro card."

"Don't get so cocky. Do those people put the bed together when they come?"

"Of course," he said. "Want some pizza?"

"No, I'm trying to scare up some work. Making calls."

"Okay, see you later," and he left.

I wasn't really trying to scare up work, although I should have been. I was figuring out how to make the life I wanted work. I was figuring out how to earn a living in a way that suited me.

And, one day, if it was meant to happen, it would be Arieh who would ring my buzzer and arrive at my door with a ring and make a life with me, in my new bed, away from his bizarre bed. He would come up the stairs with positiveness. No more talk of how everything was over. He would be able to create. I was trying to move myself toward that.

And, if he didn't come to my door, I would find someone who would. Someone I loved, as the Rabbi said. Someone I loved because they treated me well. Arieh had given me that.

One day that would happen.

ABOUT THE AUTHOR

British born, Montreal raised, New York City honed, JACQUELINE GAY WALLEY, under the pen name GAY WALLEY, has been publishing short stories since 1988 and published her first novel, *Strings Attached*, with University Press of Mississippi (1999), which was a Finalist for the Pirates Alley/Faulkner Award and earned a Writer's Voice Capricorn Award and the Paris Book Festival Award. *The Erotic Fire of the Unattainable: Aphorisms on Love, Art and the Vicissitudes of Life* was published by IML Publications in 2007 and was reissued by Skyhorse Publishing 2015. This book, *The Erotic Fire of the Unattainable* was a finalist for the Paris Book Festival Award and from this, she wrote a screenplay for the film, *The Unattainable Story* (2016) with actor, Harry Hamlin, which premiered at the Mostra Film Festival in Sao Paolo, Brazil. Walley also wrote a screenplay for director Frank Vitale's docufiction feature film, *Erotic Fire of the Unattainable: Longing to be Found* (2020), which was featured in Brooklyn Film Festival, Sarasota Film Festival, Cinequest Film & Creativity Festival in San Jose, ReadingFilmFest, and American Fringe in Paris (2020). Her novel, *Lost in Montreal* (2013) was published by Incanto Press, along with the novel, *Duet*, which was written with Kurt Haber. Walley's e-books, *How to Write Your First Novel, Save Your One Person Business from Extinction*, and *The Smart Guide to Business Writing* are featured on Bookboon, as well as *How to Keep Calm*

and Carry on Without Money and *How to be Beautiful* available on Amazon. In 2013, her play *Love, Genius and a Walk* opened in the Midtown Festival, New York, and was nominated for 6 awards including best playwright, in 2018, it also played in London at The Etcetera Theatre above The Oxford Arms pub as well as at three other pub theatres. It is scheduled to open in 2021 in Theatro Techni in London. October 2021, Jacqueline Gay Walley's 6 novel *Venus as She Ages Collection: Strings Attached* (second edition, under her pen name, Gay Walley), *To Any Lengths*, *Prison Sex*, *The Bed You Lie In*, *Write She Said*, and *Magnetism*, is being launched worldwide through IML Publications, distributed by Ingram.

Since IML's humble erratic beginnings, the mascot, which has reverently danced across our newsletter, the watermarks of the website, the original interiors, and now these front and back pages, is a graphic symbol of the Kalahari San Bushmen's Trickster God, the praying mantis, who has forever—or for as long as they can remember—been inspiring the mythological stories of these First People who nomadically walk the earth whenever they can, as our nomad authors write their way through life.